The Bystander's Scrapbook

Joseph Torra is the author of *Gas Station*, *Tony Luongo* and *My Ground*, along with *Keep Watching the Sky*, a collection of poetry. He lives in Somerville, Massachusetts.

BY THE SAME AUTHOR

Keep Watching the Sky (*poetry*)
Gas Station
Tony Luongo
My Ground

The
BYSTANDER'S
SCRAPBOOK

JOSEPH TORRA

Weidenfeld & Nicolson
LONDON

Copyright © 2001 Joseph Torra

The right of Joseph Torra to be identified as the author
of this work has been asserted by him in accordance
with the Copyright, Designs and Patents Act 1988

All rights reserved. No part of this publication may be
reproduced, stored in a retrieval system, or transmitted
in any form or by any means, electronic, mechanical,
photocopying, recording or otherwise without the prior
permission of the copyright owner

First published in Great Britain in 2001
by Weidenfeld & Nicolson
an imprint of The Orion Publishing Group
Orion House, 5 Upper St Martin's Lane,
London WC2H 9EA

A CIP catalogue record for this book
is available from the British Library

ISBN 0 575 06767 5

Typeset in Great Britain by Deltatype, Birkenhead, Merseyside
Printed and bound by
The Guernsey Press Co. Ltd, Guernsey, C.I.

'In doing of history, of writing history and teaching history, you are always selecting out of an enormous body of data, and it can only be a very, very tiny selection out of that great body of information, inevitably. And what you select, or as in most cases what is selected for you ... is dependent upon the viewpoint of the selector. And so I understood that there can be no such thing as an objective presentation of the facts from the past.'

—Howard Zinn

for Bob

■■■

I met Vin in 1984. Carol and I were living in a Queen Anne Victorian which had long since surrendered its elegance to aluminum siding, apartments, dropped-ceilings and cheap paneling. I was reading and doing research in no organized way. We worked long hours on weekend jobs; Monday through Friday, Carol and I remained close to home, except for occasional trips to New York City, while local neighborhoods gentrified and wild people from the seventies worked corporate jobs, drove BMWs, and talked about how much money they were making under the new administration.

Carol and her fellow poets were reading their way through *The Divine Comedy*, meeting at our place every Monday. The first night he came I assumed Vin was a poet. Who else would take a night off to read poetry in Italian? He thumbed through our records and commented favorably on our jazz tastes, then made snide remarks about the rock and roll. Vin was the first to read that evening, and I was struck by the pacific tone in his voice, the sensitivity and attentiveness he brought to the words *'Nel mezzo del cammin di nostra vita.'*

They read their way through most of the first Canto before an argument erupted. Luella, an angst-ridden graduate-student with wire-rimmed glasses and a long face, said she wasn't sure if she could trust Dante. Raffaelo, a good-looking man who'd already published a book of poems and had the hots for Carol said, 'What would you like, a signed fucking affidavit?' They screamed at each other until Vin intervened with a calming but lengthy commentary on the virtues of each argument. I didn't pay attention to much of what he said until he finished with the statement, 'We are, after all, the sum total of our words.' This made me sit up and take note.

We drank much wine, and ate food I brought home from work over the weekend. When the evening was over Vin shook my hand hard, his eyes slightly crossed to the lower-inside-corners through his thick and in-need-of-a-good-cleaning lenses, and he thanked us for the hospitality.

Later I recalled that we originally met over the phone when he was director of Cambridge's Dante Society, and I was looking for a space to show films on twentieth-century revolution. Carol's friend Raffaelo told me to call his friend Vin, who might help secure the Dante hall. Vin and I talked on the phone at length. He said it might work out, but at that time there were internal wars at the Dante which he hoped would be resolved. It never did happen. But Vin had seen all the films I mentioned, and suggested others. I asked him was he a historian and he said he was a historian of sorts.

After that we met occasionally for coffee and beers until our friendship was cemented in 1985 when I accompanied him on a trip to Vermont for the unveiling of a twenty-three-foot, forty-three-ton granite statue erected to commemorate the Italian immigration to Barre, Vermont. The statue was dedicated to Carlo Abate, who, during the earlier part of the century, was an artist in Barre, and founder of the first art school for monumental draftsmen and designers. It was a typical celebration with a bad marching band, vacuous speeches, and all the while Vin bemoaned the fact that there were no longer any Italians living in Barre. I was eager to meet the great anarchist and writer Harold Blatner, who lived near Barre; but when Vin phoned his old friend from the motel, we learned that the ageing and ailing Blatner had been admitted to a hospital with heart trouble and only family were allowed to visit.

Vin took me to a cemetery on the outskirts of town where a tradition of granite monuments was relegated to art form. We walked among the remains of Italian families, men who were granite workers and met early death by silicosis during a period spanning the late nineteenth through early twentieth centuries. Barely one out of five lived through thirty. Many of the workers were socialists and anarchists who migrated to Barre for work and Vermont's political tolerance. Vin was familiar with the names. Donato Brusa came from the Abbruzzi and worked with Luigi Galleani on his paper. Giuliano Bianchi was the man who got Carlo Valdinoci out of Vermont and drove him to Boston. I didn't know who Valdinoci was and Vin said Alas, so close to home. Elia Corti, Barre's celebrated carver, was shot and killed in 1903 during a gathering for socialist leader Giacinoto Serrati at Socialist Hall on Granite Street. Corti and an anarchist faction got into an argument with the socialists; a socialist tool sharpener pulled out a revolver and, shooting aimlessly, struck Corti. A life-sized statue cut a wise, contemplative, mustached Corti, sitting on the perch of a granite wall, dressed in a suit, at his feet an arrangement of the sculptor's tools including the new pneumatic drill, the base carved by grieving area stone cutters.

In the cemetery's newer section a married couple was carved into a granite bed; an oversize granite soccer ball marked the grave of a soccer lover; a corner-balanced granite cube was engraved with highlights of a deceased salesman's life; a granite race car distinguished the remains of a race-car driver killed in a snowmobile accident. The headstone of a truck driver featured a sandblasted relief of a tractor-trailer engraved with the Shell Oil company logo. Vin said we'd come a long way from anarchists to Shell Oil.

Around the town only a few of the old cutting sheds were in operation; the local granite industry had dwindled. The old socialist block once housed cooperative stores but Socialist Hall was empty and deteriorated, its red bricks crumbling, windows boarded, the arm-and-hammer granite medallion with Socialist Labor Party insignia clinging crookedly by one nail over the locked entrance. A sign said the building was currently under restoration by the Barre Historical Society.

We found the majority of the quarries abandoned, and tried to imagine the job of blasting huge pieces of granite free, cutting them into blocks and moving them by wagon and rail to the sheds where in day-long stone-dust cutters cut and processed masses of granite for the railroad cars. After a bland dinner at a local diner, we bought a bottle and retired to our room to drink room-temperature scotch out of Dixie cups.

I told Vin about leaving graduate school, and he listened intently as I explained how my mentor, the historian Frederick Quinn, and another progressive history teacher were squeezed out of the history department at Charles University. I was in the middle of my second year, soon to begin writing my dissertation on the suppression of free speech in America, second decade of the twentieth century. Without Professor Quinn as my advisor, I suddenly faced a stripped-down, conservative history department. One professor in the opposite camp told me, 'You'd better change your attitude or you're not going to fare well here.' I dropped out.

Vin said that no good could come from too much time spent in an institution. In the old days, radicals subverted institutions, now they were absorbed by them. To my surprise, Vin and Frederick Quinn were old friends. Though he never studied history formally (he'd graduated from Boston University with a math degree), Vin was as knowledgeable as any historian I knew. I'd ask a question and Vin answered with treatises, leaping from one topic to another, leaving my jaw slack. Then, after a ten, fifteen-minute or half-an-hour roll, he found his way back to my now-forgotten question. 'So you see, Gregorio, this is not a simple matter but a complicated issue with a substantial number of variables and consequences.'

Vin called me Gregorio, my birth name. With the exception of my father, everyone always called me Greg. I suppose one reason I was attracted to Vin was because of my father, who ran with women, gambled, drank and when he drank he hit my mother. I turned inward. Perhaps it was a mixed blessing for my mother to die young. I was ten. She was alone in this country. Her family had remained in Italy and my father never did anything but beat her down physically and emotionally. So I made up games about people who lived in old times.

Vin was unlike anyone I knew growing up, and he lived in the same house his entire life on a street in my old neighborhood, but we'd never crossed paths. I asked him that night in the motel room, 'Where the fuck have you been all this time?' He had fabulous thick white hair, a dandruff-laden mop, you could ski on his snow-capped shoulders. His white-dusted eyeglasses were smudged, his clothing was utilitarian, often dirty and spotted with permanent stains. Thick disheveled eyebrows garnished his round face, which was always one or two days away from a shave, his mustache grew bushy and untrimmed. Vin never married and lived downstairs from his brother, a shifty-looking guy impeccably dressed in Italian-cut clothes, well hung with gold jewelry and driving a big Buick. When I first met Vin his mother lived with him but her health was failing. Vin was short and broad shouldered, into his fifties when we met and carried extra weight from his love of food and drink. As a young man he was an athlete and played football at Somerville High but his intellectual pursuits eventually won out over his athletic ones.

On the drive home from Barre I sparked Vin's interest when I told him I was researching Herbert Minderman. Because of my former university affiliation, I once had access to the journals in the Minderman archive at Harvard. I thought Vin was putting me on when he told me he had the Minderman journals in his microfilm archive and I was welcome to them. But soon I learned the largest anarchist archive in the country sat in a twelve-by-twelve room in Vin's dilapidated two-family house on a busy Somerville street.

I went into Vin's for a nightcap and, just as he had assured me, I viewed the Minderman journals through his microfilm machine. I was readying to leave when Vin asked could I keep a secret. Of course. 'No,' he said. 'I mean really keep a secret.' If this was important, it meant that Vin trusted me. I avoided close friendships and relationships. Carol was an exception. I'd shared a lot about myself with Vin during the past two days. Curiosity aroused, I uneasily assured him that he could count on me to keep his secret.

He went to one of the metal file cabinets and opened it. He withdrew a wooden box, placed the box on his cluttered desk, unhooked a latch and lifted the lid. There was tissue wrap, which he unwrapped, revealing three small leather-bound books exactly the same size, faded dull brown. He lifted the top book and placed it into my hands. I opened it to the first page, which was handwritten in Italian, a date read January 3, 1930. The pages were dull yellow and frail, but the ink was thick and writing legible. Vin asked if I had any idea what I was holding. I didn't. He smiled a smile pointed enough to show he couldn't be more pleased. I was holding the memoirs of Errico Malatesta. But Malatesta never wrote memoirs, he lived out his late years of house arrest under Mussolini. Vin said, 'So it's been said,' but the eyes don't lie and here was proof to the contrary. He was going to translate all three books, the early, middle and late years, into English. I was now among a handful of people in the world who knew that the memoirs existed; I couldn't tell anyone, not even Carol.

September 1917, Northern Mexico

Slight rise of a desert hill backdropped by mesas. Dry creek-bed below. Three men on horseback. Dark desert-day sky's charcoal smudge on gray slate thickens black in narrow strips. Two men move east toward the coast in hopes of finding passage to South America and eventually, Italy. Carlo Valdinoci turns his horse north.

When he came to Mexico to answer the Internationalists' call, it was a time of fate. The Mexican insurrection was a model for future revolutions. If Italy entered the Great War, he would be deported or jailed. There was nothing to lose. But in time the Italians grew suspicious of the Mexican revolution. It lost touch with the peasantry and became a bourgeois revolution. The plan for land reform was nothing more than turning control from one corrupted institution over to another. The Italians will take no part in such a revolution.

Carlo waves good-bye, leads his horse down a hill across the dry creek and up another hill to a massive, sharply cut mesa. He turns to squint into the blinding sun then looks to the horizon. In the distance a blue mountain range is due north.

All day Carlo Valdinoci maintains a north-westerly route, avoiding the dust trail from a troop of American regulars off to his east. Towards evening he unpacks the horse, spreads his bedroll and in waning daylight nibbles jerky. When finished, he climbs a mass of rocks, perches, measures distant smoke from soldiers' fires. He reaches inside his jacket for a pocket sewn in the liner; the last time he saw his mother, she sewed it there. He removes a leather fold. Inside it a ten-dollar bill and a photograph. She walked him away from Salvatore, pulled the ten-dollar bill from inside her dress, placed it in his hand.

Stick to the rails and out of sight. The struggle is over for now. The nations are too strong and established powers too entrenched. The Mexicans are unable to see their folly. Many good men and women will die. Despite Zapata and Villa nothing will change.

He holds the photograph against the final light. Tina's dark hair brushed and pinned-up, small birthmark spotting the upper left-hand side of a willful forehead, eyes staring straight into the camera. Carlo is dressed in a suit, short, broad-shouldered, thick head of hair, crooked-toothed smile, bushy mustache, gazing past the camera, an over-foaming mug of ale in his hands. Next to Carlo and Tina stand Luigi and Bonita Galleani.

It was the last picnic of the East Boston Group before it disbanded and its members went in hiding or to Mexico. Carlo and Giovannitti made speeches that day. And when Galleani made his speech people were shouting and cheering, he worked them up into a frenzy. They cried when he finished, as if the world would be different the next day.

September 1917, Bentham, Massachusetts

Giulia shaded her eyes and looked across the recently harvested field. Any day he would arrive and he would be hungry. If he came by automobile she would hear him first. But he would come the back way. Salvatore was angry when he heard Carlo was returning. Carlo was a trouble-maker and if people listened to the likes of him, they would go around killing and robbing each other. Salvatore did everything he could to keep his name from being connected with Carlo's; but having never had children of his own, he could only guess at the extent to which people go for their offspring. He was, however, certain how unconditionally Giulia was capable of loving.

She walked to the pump, filled a bucket and made several trips from the pump to the black steel pot hanging in the shed's fireplace. When the pot was full enough, she broke straw and kindled a fire which she fueled to a higher pitch with a split hardwood log. She reached for her knife and walked to a large overturned straw basket, bent over it and lifted a corner enough to allow the first of two chickens to stick out its head. In the corner of the shed over a gravel bed she turned the desperately fluttering chicken upside down and held its backside firmly between her two legs, she gripped its head with her left hand, the neck fully exposed, and cut deep with her knife. The chicken jerked wildly, blood spurted to heart beats and pump-by-pump it decreased until everything was still. She shook the bird, wriggled its neck to rid it of the last drops of blood, and repeated the procedure on the second chicken. Then she brought the dead birds to the boiling water, dropped them in for an instant to loosen the feathers for skinning and placed them upon a wooden butcher's block. With a fire poker she lifted the water bucket by its handle and carefully carried the pot to the gravel bed where she placed it down and turned the boiling water on to the bloody gravel.

There were potatoes, onions, carrots and squash. The mushrooms she picked were never like they were back home, though yesterday she picked a giant hen-of-the woods, the best eating of all the mushrooms here. She would make dough and cut macaroni. When he got there he would be hungry.

The Notebooks

'. . . On February 18 agents of the Federal Government forced their way into the office of *Regeneracion*, the revolutionary weekly of the Mexican Liberal Party, published in Los Angeles, and brutally beat up and arrested the editors of the paper, Ricardo and Enrique Flores Magon . . . They are men of rare type seldom produced outside of Russia and Mexico: men who have sacrificed social position, comfort and personal safety for the cause of the people . . . Present-day America has failed to evolve such superior types of social consciousness . . . A double task faced them: to educate and organize the Mexican people into an effective weapon of revolution and, still more important – and more difficult – to enlighten the American people to the real issues involved in the Mexican uprising . . . And now it is the learned academician in the White House who is hastening to the aid of Carranza and Wall Street, to suppress the work of *Regeneracion*. They will try again to send the Magons to the penitentiary. We call on all rebels and fair-minded people not to permit this outrage . . . Many of us came to America with no clear idea of *la questione sociale*. But we learn pretty quick that America was no bed of roses. We saw the greed. It was not that we did not have greed in the old country; but in America the great size of the greed and the greater hypocrisy to justify it took our breaths away. They beat us down at first, but our time would come. The Lawrence Strike of 1912, that was our moment. It was not enough that those owners made life so expensive our women and children had to work in order to live; but they stole pennies out of our paychecks by legal trickery. *Senza Vergogna* . . . Luigi Galleani was our inspiration. We called him El Vecc, he could speak to a handful of workers, or thousands. And what a voice he had. Even those who did not speak Italian – Armenians, Jews, Poles, Germans and French-Canadians – went crazy after they heard him. It was like Giuseppe Verdi: the passion would sweep right through you. And El Vecc's ideas became *pericoloso*, dangerous to the authorities. He never stepped back, and he was always respected, even by his enemies. He believed we could make a new world . . .'

from The Journals of Herbert Minderman, 1912:

Today they took our blankets and pillows. We are so many in the cell we must sleep in shifts of four hours per day each man. The excrement bucket has not been emptied in three days and each day more prisoners are squeezed into the cells. In court the prisoners demand their right to trial and defend themselves, challenging the jury system every step of the way. It is said that a good prisoner can strangle the court for the whole day. The courts are able to process ten cases a week while dozens are arrested each day. As soon as one speaker is hauled off the soapbox, another is eager to climb and continue the battle. We sing and shout out to each other from our cells. We held a meeting of the Local 66. Then we sang in unison. The guards came and told us to be quiet. We sang louder. The guards returned and they tied and gagged a man with his own sock. We counter-attacked with a battleship: non-stop noise. Yelling, banging on the cell bars and floors. Songs and cheers, slogans and jeers. In response to our battleship the guards came to remove and isolate those men who they believe to be our leaders. The men were marched to the yard and ordered to kiss the American flag and sing 'The Star Spangled Banner'. All of them refused. The guards made them run the gauntlet and they were beaten by clubs and pick handles. Once again the men were ordered to kiss the American flag and sing 'The Star Spangled Banner'. But they refused. They were beaten at will. Only one of the two men taken from my cell was returned. He was bloody and barely conscious. One guard told us the other man was taken to the hospital but Sam Tell, the beaten man, believes otherwise. This afternoon four new prisoners were squeezed into our cell. They told us the strike is alive and the spirits of the Local 66 on the outside are high. But city officials are using vigilantes to break the strike. The vigilantes patrol the city borders and the railroad yards where strike supporters trickle in. On first warning they make threats. But any man who attempts to pass through the vigilante line is beaten bloody and turned back.

The Memoirs of Errico Malatesta, Early Years

January 3, 1930

The professional historian may prefer to present the fruits of his research as sensational events, large-scale conflicts between nations and classes, wars, revolutions, the ins and outs of diplomacy and conspiracies; but what is really much more significant are the innumerable daily contacts between individuals and between groups which are the true substance of social life.

On my front porch there is a permanent police post with a guard day and night. If anyone should come to see me they are arrested. If I try to go out in public, any person who approaches me is arrested. I rarely receive mail, or if I do, it has been opened and examined. My companion and my daughter are followed everywhere they go. Sometimes, I wish that I had listened to Fabbri and the others and left Italy while there was time.

I have witnessed many conflicts, crossed countless borders, watched governments tumble and lived in prison cells. I have spoken at thousands of meetings, maintained hundreds of correspondences, written more articles and manifestos than I can calculate. Half of my life I have lived in exile!

Time, dates, events, for me, have become one big knot, and all I do is pull out strands and threads. There is no longer any way I can trust the accuracy of my recollections. The memory of one event slides into another. My dreams may be real. What is real, may be dreams.

I begin with the insurrection of 1877. I'm standing on the steps at the ruins of Castello del Vento in the southern Italian countryside, prying the top off a wooden case full of carbine rifles. In past times members of the secret societies gathered on these very steps, and I launch the southern insurrection from this historic site.

Three days earlier in Taranto, the plan was for me to make contact with five hundred revolutionaries, and secure several cases of rifles sent from Naples. My first objective was to seize the railroad station in

Taranto, leave a troop of revolutionaries to guard it, then move on to the Castello with the rest of the men. But only two men were at the railroad station to greet me; so I hid the rifles in a hotel room, and, realizing we were only three, the other two men ran off. I removed the rifles, tied them on to a horse's back and made the fifty-mile trip to the ruins alone on foot. In the end, I had to shoot the horse.

A call is out for Internationalists to gather at the ruins, and I expect several hundred men; but there are only four, and each of them dressed in the red and black emblem of the International. I hand each man a shiny new rifle, raise my gun in the air and shout, 'Death to the Perfect!'

In Florence, the plan was to massacre the authorities at 2 a.m.; but, at 2 a.m. the city was silent. Bakunin himself slept with a pistol under his pillow, and he escaped the authorities by disguising himself as an old street woman.

In Bologna, someone alerted the authorities in advance, and many comrades were arrested in their beds. During the night, a fire was to be lit as a diversion in the center of the city, and the workers' organizations would man the barricades. They would capture the National Guard armory, the rifles and ammunition, then march on the banks and the gas works! Someone informed the police, who found the plot so ridiculous they did not believe the anarchists were serious.

Four hundred men amassed outside of Bologna to act as a reserve wherever needed; but several days passed and they never received orders, so leaders dispersed the group, and many men returned to Bologna, and into the waiting hands of the police.

A thousand men were gathered in the Abbruzzi. Or one hundred, armed with a few carbines, pistols and knives. In the hills inland from Rome a small band of Internationalists skirmished with the army for days, carrying out an effective guerrilla war in the countryside, raiding villas, putting out landlords, turning the land over to the peasants and breaking into banks.

Despite the failures in the north, the state is weak. The civil war left much of the political structure in the south in disarray, and on the brink of tottering. I tell the men the time is ripe for an uprising, it will spark a larger general insurrection all over the rest of Italy, and bring the state down.

The Notebooks

'... Nature has done more for Somerville than for any of our sister cities in the gift of charming hills, beautiful in outline, graceful in slope, easy of ascent and fortunately connected. To these hills the better class of community inevitably tend. There seems to be a law of residence as of morals that the best go upon the heights eventually, as the lower classes trench upon their lowland territory ... It is claimed by some persons that the existence of such industries within the limits of our city has a tendency to vitiate the atmosphere, to endanger the public health, and to keep away from the city *a class of people whose presence would be very desirable* ... it is the wage earners shut up daily in dark stores and dingy work rooms and the children of the poorer classes compelled to live in crowded, ill-vented tenements who will derive greatest benefit from the pure air and beautiful scenery of our public reservations, and it is our duty to see to it that their needs are not neglected ... C.H. Guild, Esq. has bought a fine estate in Newton Highlands and will move there soon. Somerville will part company with Mr Guide with feelings of deep regret ... Somerville has some fine old houses, but for the most part their broad domains of former days have been encroached on until, in many places, they look cramped without the elbow room and breathing space which aristocratic respectability requires ...'

Diary of Christina Donato:

'I sleep when I can. The morning sounds of wagons and trucks and shouts along Somerville Avenue I dull by draping a blanket over the window. Often the street noises keep me awake, and after hours of tossing, I rise to transact business, work on an article or typeset. The airplanes flying over are most annoying; though they are among us scarcely a decade, I do not remember the time before them. We raid at night. Working from tips, we learn of an unlocked boxcar door, an open door of a warehouse or an unattended truck. There are automobiles parked outside restaurants and clubs, we take anything left behind; if nothing, we jack the automobiles up and steal the tires. During holiday and vacation season, the affluent are away and their staffs with them. Valuables are often locked, but a silver letter opener or a gold fountain pen are left out in a den, a silverware or crystal set in a dining room, a pocket watch in the drawer of a night table. Everything goes to the movement; we keep only enough for rent and groceries. There are arguments over how money from the loot should be divided; how much should go to the movement and how much should remain in our hands. It's the same people who want more to line their pockets and the same ones who are willing to settle for what they need to see them through. I do not allow the men to condescend to me; and I make certain that I perform any tasks they do. Being smaller and lighter means I move quicker, climb higher and squeeze through openings the men cannot.'

Government Trying to Break I.W.W.'s Back

Determined to check I.W.W. membership, last week federal agents raided I.W.W. halls across the nation with warrants for the arrests of all present and past I.W.W. leaders on grounds that they have conspired to disrupt the war effort. At the time of this writing it is not clear who and how many have been arrested. Big Bill Haywood, one of the first to be arrested in Chicago, is calling for a mass trial for all.

President Wilson and The Department of Justice, under the heavy hand of Attorney General Palmer, are determined to use the I.W.W.'s stand against the war to undermine and destroy the I.W.W. once and for all. During the raids the federal agents confiscated records, correspondences and other literature.

This increased government aggression can be traced back to the recent arrests and jailing of Emma Goldman and Alexander Berkman, and the arrests of the 450 leaders of the Green Corn Rebellion who planned to march on Washington (eating green corn all the way) to show opposition to the capitalist war. When Wilson signed the Espionage Act, the United States made it clear that freedom of speech will have its limit.

As I write more people around the country are being jailed for expressing their opinions. The war is not about freedom, except for the powers-that-be to continue their control at the cost of freedom for others.

– Rossa Nero

■ ■ ■

Carol and I purchased our first computer and Vin walked us through the process. We had little furniture and a lot of space in that Central Street apartment so we put the computer and printer on a table in the dining room. The room had a high ceiling, bay windows and a view out to the Boston skyline; with our new technological addition, we called it the command post.

Vin said the computer was modern man's plow, and it should be used only as a tool. Carol wanted to start a poetry magazine. Vin knew what we needed to know, and he supplied us with updated versions of programs. Vin had Boston University, MIT, and Harvard IDs, with access to all of their libraries and museums. One of his cards allowed him access to Harvard computer rooms; any software that Harvard had, Vin had. If Harvard updated a program, within days Vin updated his programs, then his friends' programs. Once he was helping Carol with the first issue of her magazine and there was a problem. He dialed a Harvard computer center number and when a person answered Vin began questioning them until his problem was solved. I asked him how he got away with it and he said as far as the person on the other end of the phone knew, they were talking to a professor on an inside line.

As long as I knew him Vin never had a job and he claimed never to have paid income tax. He was writing a book, though I never saw a page from it. He spent immeasurable time at the libraries of Harvard, Boston University, or the Boston Public Library's Rare Book Room, from where he might call me mid-afternoon to meet later for coffee where he'd produce photocopies of documents, letters or pages from some rare manuscripts, and removing them from his overflowing briefcase begin *in medias res*, 'So this is a series of letters from Carlo Tresca to Franco Sarcia, I told you about Franco, he was one of the Sicilians, a musician, who was deported along with Galleani and, as it turns out, his sister is said to have been lovers with, well, lovers, if you can call it that, she was a spirited woman and in those days the spirit of free love was in the air. When I found that sheaf of letters in the Dante archives, there were several letters from Sarcia's sister to Valdinoci, and, I must say, they were rather dicey, some very explicit language. Well. And as it turns out when Valdinoci was in New York along with Galleani and Sarcia, it looks like Valdinoci might have had an affair with Sarcia's sister who was also lovers with Tresca and was deported along with Sarcia. Galleani of course hid out in Vermont for several years and wasn't deported until after the war. But I don't think anyone at the Dante Library even knows these letters are there. I would have taken them but the son-of-a-bitch new director was watching me like a hawk, so I had all I could do to photocopy them.'

Vin loved to walk along Somerville Avenue and listen to the medley of languages spoken in the span of several blocks amongst denizens of body shops, vinyl-sided tenements, store-front-converted apartments, bars, gas stations, sub shops and grocers. He called it a life-line to the planet. Someone invariably jacked up an old car on the sidewalk to remove a transmission or rear end. Spanish music, Island music, Indian music, African music, rock and roll and rap swelled from boom boxes, radios of passing cars and apartment windows, while in warm weather exotic spices sprayed the air. We hung out at an unpretentious café on Somerville Avenue, next door from Son of God Auto Body. They made good espresso and the owner was a dark woman, a mix of Italian and Greek. She never offered a smile to anyone. The mayor might be sitting at a table with a librarian, local musicians drinking large mugs, young would-be poets writing in notebooks, Leo the electrician, Gus the plumber or auto body workers from Son of God.

One day Vin appeared with a photocopied government file list of suspected communists, over one hundred pages long, with the usual suspects like Julius and Ethel Rosenberg, but others like Sinatra and Elvis. Alongside each name was a number listing the page length of each file. Vin was fascinated with the article and had already studied and marked it extensively with a pencil. Another day he came across a rare post-trial document from the Sacco and Vanzetti case on which he often wrote and lectured. He was following a lead (he always was following a lead which might unearth a speck information to help him with his puzzle) and came upon the document quite by accident. Vin slipped it in his briefcase.

I never understood how his pieces fitted together. If I asked him exactly what kind of book he was writing, Vin loosely implied that it had to do with the history of Italian-American anarchism. He was especially interested in the Sacco and Vanzetti trial, but he never gave me a straight answer when I asked him if he thought Sacco and Vanzetti were guilty or innocent. Gregorio, Gregorio he would say, it's not that simple, and he'd expound at length about the various aspects of the trial, who the men were supposed to be and who the men were not, what role the media played in the trial, what effect their portrayal of the two men, what role the defense and prosecution, what role public support and opinion which may or may not have hindered in their receiving a fair trial. But what concerned Vin was not Sacco and Vanzetti's innocence or guilt, but whether they received a fair trial. Vin knew all the survivors of the Sacco and Vanzetti family. Over the decades he'd interviewed every person involved with the case and he'd uncovered nuggets which had been overlooked by previous research mostly because they were written in Italian, or, more specifically, Italian dialect.

Vin believed that nothing original could be written about the case, and everything that could be said, one way or another, had already been said. What he might do was put everything that had been said into a new perspective. Because there was no other way to say what was, perhaps he could find a new way to say what wasn't. Provisional history was only endless revisions which got to be like trying to turn an ocean liner. Vin didn't want that. There was just a little more information to gather in order to bring his book into full light, and that last bit of information might be just around the corner.

But he would never have *all* the information; no matter how many documents and letters he accumulated or sources he tapped, there would be missing pieces, inaccurate information. I was speaking as much to myself. Long before my mentors had been forced out of Charles University, I'd secretly given up on formal history, writing a dissertation and teaching. It had become an endless mass of information and I had no sense of how to use the rare and not-so-rare documents, second, third and fourth-hand stories, letters, diaries, journals. What truth was in any of it and how much was simply guessing, fictionalizing, or serving the needs of specific agendas? What difference fiction or fact?

All the difference in the world to Vin. Fiction was for entertainment. History was for shaping the future of the world. If you distorted history, you distorted the future. Vin said historians should be imaginative, but must stick as close to the facts as possible. Fiction writers could depend on their imagination and do as they please with facts. He abhorred history which concerned itself with dominant classes, and failed to acknowledge that history should deal with the people as a whole. Historians too often were simple chroniclers who feigned impartiality and avoided real interpretation of the past. For Vin, a true historian had the great responsibility of teaching present day human beings who they are and how their society had become what it is. Under such circumstances, a chronicler was of no use. Indeed my own experiences had confirmed that a formal academic study of history showed little tolerance for a historic inquiry that endeavored beyond mere chronicling.

The Memoirs of Errico Malatesta, Early Years

How can I lead an insurrection with a handful of men? And how can I trust these four men sleeping so soundly, they snore in unison from the outlying rooms? Any of them could be spies.

I lift my head up and look out the window at stars brilliant in the black sky. The air is cool and dry; it is good for my lungs, I take deep breaths and drop my head. The sounds of the snores envelop my consciousness and I am seduced. Several times I fall off to sleep, but my mind wakes itself up. I reach for the pistol in the field bag to my left, certain I know the location of its handle.

We are outnumbered. I spread the men along a hill above a burning village. Army regulars storm up the ridge, and we stave them off. One of the men takes a bullet in the back of the head as regulars are above us and firing down. The dead man is lying in dirt face up, forehead blown out by an exiting bullet, and his face slowly transforms into the face of my father on his deathbed, those glazed eyeballs turned upward, the tongue pointing out from the corner of his mouth like a carcass hanging on a butcher's hook.

The regulars descend upon us and we run for the wooded area to the left of our entrenchment. Bullets fly and ricochet; several lodge in my back and legs. I reach the wooded area with blood pumping from my wounds and run until I drop into a small stream. The forest is shrouded with smoke. I hear shooting and shouting.

I wake during the night to a full moon lighting the forest. My wounds are clotted over. There is a noise in the brush and I duck to see a riderless horse walking towards me. The horse stops and I reach for its mane to pull myself up but the horse's hair pulls out in my hands, his skin is flayed off and the flesh is a bloody gelatin.

The Notebooks

'. . . My "crime" consists not in giving the information, but solely on the advocacy of birth control. There are three indictments, based on twelve articles, eleven of which are for *printing the words* "prevention of conception". To the elect of federal officialdom these words themselves are considered lewd, lascivious and obscene. In none of these articles is any information given – simply discussions of the subject addressed to working women of this country . . . Many "radical" advisers have assured me that the wisest course for me to follow in fighting the case would be to plead "guilty" to this "obscenity", and to throw myself upon the mercy of the court, which could mean, according to those familiar with the administration of "justice", a light sentence or a small fine . . . It is unfortunate that so many radicals and so-called revolutionaries have failed to understand that my object in this work has been to remove, or to try to remove, the term "prevention of conception" from this section of the penal code, where it has been labeled by our wise legislators as "filthy, vile and obscene", and not to obtain deserved currency for this valuable idea and practice . . . The problem of staying out of jail or getting put into jail is merely incidental to this fight . . . The first step in the birth control movement, or any other propaganda requiring a free press, is to open the mails to the people of this country, *regardless of class*. Nothing can be accomplished without the free and open discussion of the subject . . . When my case is called in the federal courts, probably next month, I shall enter a plea of "not guilty", in order to separate the idea of prevention of conception and birth control from the sphere of pornography, from the gutter of slime and filth where the lily-livered legislators have placed it . . .'

28 Arrested Under Espionage Act Face Up To 20 Years

Twenty-four men and four women were arrested last week at a meeting of the Boston branch of the No-Conscription League. An estimated one hundred League members were in attendance but many managed to escape through a hidden door which leads to a stairway and a neighboring building.

The twenty-four arrested are being held without bail. If convicted, the men and women could face up to twenty years each in prison under the terms of President Wilson's Espionage Act. Two of the No-Conscription League's founders, Emma Goldman and Alexander Berkman, were recently arrested in New York City. This is the first case in Boston of anti-war activists being arrested under the Espionage Act.

In Philadelphia, Charles Schenck, the first person in the country to be arrested for violating the Espionage Act, has been sentenced to six months in prison. Schenck will appeal the verdict and take the matter to the Supreme Court. Schenck was arrested only one week after the Espionage Act went into effect for distributing leaflets denouncing the draft and the war.

As Schenck's pamphlet pointed out, the Conscription Act is 'a monstrous deed against humanity in the interest of the financiers of Wall Street.' We must not fall victim to the propaganda of the major newspapers and newsreels portraying the Germans as baby killing anti-Christs. The president who was elected on a promise to keep the country out of war is now in the pockets of the financiers. His shifting sands policy is based on power and economics. In the words of Charles Schenck: 'Do not submit to intimidation.'

– Rossa Nero

October 1, 1917

Giulia sat by the kitchen window, eyes fixed on the white pillow case. Working her needle in and out, she reached the end of her thread, stripped another stretch off her spool and threaded it on to the needle. Finished with the last petal on a flower, she began embroidering a stem down the length of the pillow case. The marriage of Mrs Polansky's son was three days away on Sunday. Giulia had one more pillow case to finish and the bedspread and pillow cases would be complete, making a fine wedding gift. She and Mrs Polansky were friends since the first day Giulia and Salvatore moved into the farm and Mrs Polansky walked the two and a half miles from her farm to introduce herself. Their husbands were never friendly towards each other. Salvatore hated the Poles. Mr Polansky hated the Italians. Salvatore had gone so far as forbid Giulia from seeing Mrs Polansky. Giulia paid his command no mind.

The women had much in common, both being widows with children from their first marriages and limited options in their home countries. Rumors were rampant in Giulia's village. Though she walked with her head high she felt the weight of women's stares and whispers. One woman accused Giulia of flirting with her husband, and spat in her face in public.

Salvatore came through San Sossio once a week selling fish. Every Friday afternoon Giulia went to the village square when she heard his ringing bell. Salvatore never married and was several years younger than Giulia. Some women speculated he was the type of man who didn't like women. Lucia DiGrigorio, the woman who spat in Giulia's face, claimed that Salvatore had lost his member in a freak accident, and what woman would want such a man? Giulia never noticed him in any particular way, and spoke with him only to transact business. One particular afternoon, several months after Luigi was killed when his wagon overturned, Giulia was paying Salvatore for a piece of fish and he told her how sorry he was to hear about what happened to her husband. She thanked hm for his condolences, and noticed his eyes were warm gray-blue.

Having embroidered the stem down the right side of the pillow case, Giulia re-threaded her needle and began the narrow leaflets, one to the left and one to the right at the bottom of the stem. She could tell by the position of the sun the last time she glanced out the window that it was mid-afternoon. Salvatore was at work at the leather tannery eight miles away. He didn't like having to take work off the farm, but the last two years had not paid off. No matter how much corn, cabbage or squash he raised, the market never offered enough of a return for his efforts. The last time Carlo stayed with them he told Salvatore that it was another example of how the capitalist system works against the farmer. Salvatore said he was fortunate to find work outside the farm. Giulia finished the second leaflet and tied off the knot. She looked out the window and thought she saw a figure along the edge of the field but it was a deer grazing.

'Hobo' Frank Little Lynched

Long-standing I.W.W. member and agitator Frank 'Hobo' Little was found dead at the end of a rope last week in Butte, Montana. Little had been in Butte since August in support of the striking copper miners. It has been reported that vigilantes hired by the local mining company lynched the ailing Little and left him dangling on a railroad trestle on the outskirts of Butte.

To those familiar with the struggle for freedom, the name Frank Little needs no introduction. For 20 years Little was at the forefront of conflicts for a better world wherever he was needed. He was at the vanguard of the free speech fights in Spokane, San Diego and Fresno. He led migrant workers, harvesters, miners and construction workers in their quest for rights in over a dozen states. No man suffered more jailings, beatings and broken bones than Frank Little while at the same time advocating peaceful direct action.

Little's long time friend and I.W.W. leader James P. Cannon has written, 'He was always for the revolt, for the struggle, for the fight. Wherever he went he "stirred up trouble" and organized the workers to rebel. He was a blood brother to all insurgents the world over.'

Police in Butte, Montana have done nothing to investigate Little's death. Thus they have proven once again that the established order, including police, the business community, local officials and big government are determined to keep the masses at their mercy with the least amount of human rights that can be afforded.

But Frank Little's name will live on in the minds of every person who imagines a world of freedom and dignity for all. A memorial will be held at the I.W.W. Hall in Somerville on Thursday night, October 23, at 7:30 P.M. To be continued.

– Rossa Nero

The Memoirs of Errico Malatesta, Early Years

I cling to the top of the telegraph pole. From this height I can see small villages at junctures of roads in every direction. The sun rises behind the hill to the east, and, already, the people are in the fields, or on the roads in donkey carts full of hay and vegetables. The sweet perfume of grapes drifts in the warm breeze.

If all goes according to plan, this year, the peasants will reap the full benefits of all their work. I remove the cutters from my belt and cut the telegraph wires. In the north-west there is a village nestled below an estate, there are several escape routes into the countryside.

What is so wrong with wanting to replace hatred with love, competition with solidarity, lies with truths? This feeling is the love of mankind, and the fact of sharing the sufferings of others. During my life I may have been right, I may have been wrong, but I avoided the fashions of each period, and this enabled me to remain free of dogmatism, and of any pretension of possessing an absolute social truth.

There is never a perfect solution for every problem at every given time. What matters is that the people, all people, should lose their sheeplike instincts and habits with which their minds have been inculcated by an age-long slavery, and that they should learn to think and act freely. It is to this great task of spiritual liberation that I devote myself.

Southern Italy, 1877

Marina sits at her window embroidering a white blanket. Her daughter Giulia sits on her lap. Giulia watches her mother intently work the blue-threaded needle in and out of the white material. Marina hums and rocks Giulia. She hears voices in the village growing louder and pays it no mind until she hears her husband Gaetano and her son Oreste. By the time she reaches the village square, several dozen local men and women are gathered in a circle. Giulia in arms, Marina edges her way in. Several armed strangers are surrounded by the villagers.

'What good is your paper?' Gaetano asks the strangers. The poster nailed to a post bears the heading DEATH TO THE PERFECT followed by a list of ten points of revolutionary ideas. 'None of these people can read!'

'Why not?' Errico Malatesta replies. 'Have you ever asked yourself why you cannot read?'

'It is not our place to read. We have work to do.'

'It is time to take your destiny into your own hands. A new day for Italy has arrived. Put your landlords out and let this harvest season be the birth of the rest of your lives. You tend the animals. You grow and press the olives and grapes, raise and harvest fruits and nuts and vegetables. And for what? So that all your efforts can be carted off to the villa on the hill?'

There is much confusion amongst the villagers. Everything that Errico Malatesta says must pass through several translations since none of the villagers speak the same dialect as the strangers. The villagers don't believe what they are hearing. Never have they heard such statements in public. During the winter months when the food supply has nearly run out and the families are reduced to bone-broth, bread and vinegary wine, one entertained the thought that it is not right that the landlord eats plenty while children grow sick with hunger. But to hear such ideas expressed in public is something new.

Standing in front of her mother little Giulia stares at the short, red-haired man trying to ignite the villagers. He's speaking words she cannot understand. Malatesta sees her watching him and walks over to pick her up. He holds her over his head. 'For the children. For the future of Italy and the world.'

Giulia laughs. She can see the whole configuration of villagers from her new vantage point, she wails her arms and legs.

A startled Marina runs to the center of the circle, kicks Malatesta in the shins and grabs Giulia from his arms. Malatesta's comrades are uneasy. They have remained mostly silent up to now, but the village men, many with pitchforks and axes in hand, are beginning to act threatening.

'Go back to where you came from,' Gaetano says. 'You can do little but cause us trouble here.'

Others agree. 'Go back where you came from. Leave us to our work.'

'I can set you free. It is up to you. Take the harvest stores into your own hands. Put your landlord out and this winter eat well and warm yourselves over fires lit by the wood of his home. You have the real power and capabilities. Do not deny them.'

Oreste tells a boy to run to the master's house and tell him to call on the police.

The four men urge Malatesta to retreat before it is too late. They run for a stone wall, climb over it and make their way for the hillside. Malatesta turns back, 'Demand and seize your freedom,' and he slips into a grove of olive trees and up over the hilltop.

'Nothing but common robbers.'

'Thieves.'

Diary of Christina Donato:

'The fence despises our politics, and threatens to turn us in and do society a favor; but he makes too much profit from our transactions. Filthy Irish scum Fillipo calls him. After our visit to the fence, we convene at a tavern in the meat-packing district. Workers come and go in their bloody shoes and bloodstained clothes, drinking coffee, beer and eating sandwiches. Each morning the tavern crew sweeps up and puts down fresh sawdust, but by late afternoon the smell of animal blood and sawdust fills the room along with strong coffee, cooking hams and tobacco smoke. The smoke hangs heavily in the air and my eyes burn. I am frequently the only woman in the tavern, and sometimes there is talk. Fillipo, Ricardo, Antonio and I disagree over how the funds should be distributed. We keep the minimum for ourselves, and the rest we hand over to the cause. There is more of a need than ever for funds now that the government is squeezing the movement from all sides. Antonio and Ricardo argue that we should keep a larger cut since we are the ones who do take all the risks. Fillipo and I are firm, and we distribute the money as we always have.'

∎∎∎

During my undergraduate years I attended the defunct Boston State College by day and worked as a waiter nights. I was appalled by the amount of food that was thrown away by the kitchen. Piles of mashed potatoes, vegetables, bottom-of-pot soup, slightly dried desserts, unused bread, the tail-end of a standing rib roast or pieces of chicken. Added to this was food left on diners' plates waiters cleared from tables. It was the seventies, when the homeless were not at the forefront of the mainstream media, but it seemed simple to me that if you took the amount of food that was tossed into the dumpster at the end of a given night, multiplied that by the thousands of restaurants across the country, a hell of a lot of food was going to waste.

Some waiters were disgusted by the idea of eating off a stranger's plate. But I was in college and on the run, famished by the end of a shift, so it made sense to grab that second uneaten pork chop or piece of chicken. If there was wine remaining in a bottle, why not indulge in a glass? I kept choice cuts of leftover meat in a doggy bag during the night, then visited the kitchen after kitchen's-closed and stocked up; I corked the remains of wine in bottles and brought everything to my studio apartment on the Fenway. All this came to a halt when I was later accepted to the Ph.D. program at Charles with a modest but full stipend. Elated, I decided never to wait on tables again. But I had to learn to live on submarine sandwiches.

As during my undergraduate years, I did no socializing my first year at Charles. Early in my second year I started hanging out with a guy in the history department who persuaded me to go to a party with him. I attended one party in all my years at college and graduate school, and I met Carol.

She was conversing with men mostly, and alternately going to the stereo to change the music someone had just put on. Later she said she watched me sitting nervously in a corner chair, rising only to use the bathroom and refill my beer cup at the tap. I hardly spoke to anyone. When I left, my associate had his shirt off and was dancing with two girls while twirling his shirt in the air. Carol and I found ourselves searching for our coats in a coat-pile and passed small talk. I noticed that she wore a black motorcycle leather too. We were walking down the stairs and she told me she was on her way to see the Real Kids at the Rat. I said nothing. They were one of my favorite local bands. At the bottom of the stairs, I stiffened to say nice to have met you, and she asked did I feel like rockin' out?

At the Rat I switched over to Jack Daniel's. So did she. It was crowded and smoky, Thundertrain ripped through a cover of 'Round and Round'. Disco was all the fashion, but Carol knew more about the local rock bands than I did. She did her undergraduate work at New York University, and while in Manhattan she frequented C.B.G.B. She asked me to dance and I told her not yet. I loved music, but a dancer I wasn't. We ordered another round and as the bourbon and beers took hold I began to feel more relaxed. I drank the second quickly and ordered a third. Shouting over the music Carol told me about her work as an x-ray technician, the punk scene in New York, and how, with her MFA in poetry from Boston University, she wanted to teach writing at a university when she published a book.

By the time the Real Kids kicked in with 'Better Be Good' I'd finished my third drink and without a word took Carol's arm and dragged her out on to the tiny dance floor. There was bumping and kids jumping up-and-down doing the Pogo. I was drunk enough not to care about how badly I looked and the music pounded great throbs through my eardrums as I attempted my usual limp-moves-in-place but it would not suffice. Carol was the most curious dancer I'd ever seen. She moved all of her body parts continually, jerking her arms, legs, back, hips, neck, head and hands as she roamed the entire room, taking strange steps, springing from one point to another; when she came to a wall or the bar she turned and proceeded in different direction. Dancing with her involved chasing her around, and when I thought I cornered her, she slipped away.

We went to my place that night. And we were together every night thereafter. She wanted to know how I could be so pale for an Italian. She asked about my family and friends. What would I do when I finished school? Did I ever read Dickens, Dickinson or Whitman? What about past girlfriends? Should we go see DMZ and The Ramones at the Rat? How often did I think about what I am doing and why? Did I examine my experiences? Who influenced me the most in life? Did I ever wear anything but jeans and t-shirts and why did I call my rubber-sole canvas shoes Willies? Why did I choose history and what did they think of my black leather jacket in the history department?

I resembled my mother more than my father. But this was not true. Whenever I stood naked in front of a mirror it was my father's thin, short, round-shouldered frame – his chinless, lipless mouth, compressed pointed nose and uneventful brown eyes staring back. I wasn't sure how often I think about what I am doing and why I am doing it. Sure, I examined my experiences. I didn't know who influenced me the most. Rocker Willie 'Loco' Alexander wore those canvas shoes and I called them Willies and once a year bought one pair of the tie-up and one pair of the slip-on. I preferred black but sometimes I got blue. I don't know why but as long as I could remember it was history because in history the past lived in the present without food, water or air. I went to my bookcase and withdrew *The Oxford History of the American People*, 1965 edition, the first book I ever purchased. I was fifteen, earned the money from an after-school job working in the market downstairs. I read it cover to cover, many times to the dismay of aunt Rose, uncle Lenny and cousin Joe. On the inside cover in green magic market I showed Carol my name and my aunt and uncle's address. It was a high-school teacher who got me to believe that my passion for history was worth something. For the most part I did poorly in school, my grades teetered on failing, but in history it was As.

Around the time I quit graduate school, Carol and I officially moved in together. I experienced mixed feelings returning to Somerville. When I left the city several years earlier I thought I could never spend another day there. But it was one of the only Boston area cities we could afford to live in. The apartment was cheap and spacious; what few furnishings we had were Carol's. Without my stipend I had to find a job, so I went to the restaurant where I once worked. There were no waiter positions available, but two dishwashers walked out and the owner said if I wanted something temporary I could work double lunch and dinner shifts on Saturday and Sunday, and he would pay me three hundred under the table. I accepted and remained there longer than I ever anticipated. Eventually, the prospect of a waiter job arose, but I had the dishwashing gig down so that I could do it with my eyes closed. No one bothered me. I listened to a radio and was content racking, rinsing, washing and stacking.

It didn't take long to get back into food foraging. The waiters were accommodating and kept doggy bags and half-full bottles of wine in the waiter station. The head chef kept things aside and Carol slowly came over to see things my way, though she was extra cautious. Because she worked in health care, she described scary scenarios of diseases we were lucky we hadn't yet caught. Carol was writing her poetry, attending readings, sending manuscripts and job applications to little magazines and colleges. I read, listened to music and drank too much as the country's social climate took a 180 degree turn.

Norfolk, Virginia, 1917

After hiding all morning Carlo Valdinoci runs for the boxcar with an open door. At a full run he is barely able to keep up. Several times he reaches for the railing but loses his footing. He digs into his lungs, gains again, wraps his hands around the railing as the train sweeps him off his feet, his legs dangling. Suddenly, two hands reach down from the boxcar, grab him under the arms and pull him aboard.

Coughing and trying to catch his breath on the platform, Carlo looks up to see a large black man standing cautiously over him. The engineer pulls the train whistle a mile ahead. Carlo nods with a smile. The man nods back.

They squat sharing the last of the stranger's bread. Clicking intervals mark the train's rumble north. Communication is done through gestures.

Carlo wonders why the man runs. Maybe K.K.K. They lynch Italians in New Orleans. Perhaps it is the black race that will lead Americans to act. If they come for us, they will go for him first ... Surely there are people who will lead this country into action. Americans will never learn to live until they learn to die.

WORKERS! Procreate Only When You Like!

From Gruppo Anarcho
Translation by Rossa Nero

Numerous families increase the misery that is great already among the poor masses of workers. The capitalist vampires, by means of the priest, morally condemn the use of scientific means in order not to have children. This they do by threatening 'hell' to those who intelligently refuse to put into the world numerous 'unlucky' (unfortunate) ones. And by means of politicians, judges, jailers they make laws, condemn and jail everybody – all those who try to diffuse among the people scientific knowledge. And indeed they tried, a short time ago, Margherita Sanger. They convicted Anderlini in the State of Illinois. A few days ago they arrested Emma Goldman in New York, and they threatened trouble to all those who have the courage to tell you the truth and let you know this practical means to prevent conception.

The Notebooks

'. . . The chief looked him over, asked, "Why?" and the boy answered this: "You know these things; you use them; why shouldn't the rest of us?" The chief's answer was short and sweet. He used three words. He said to the key turner, "Lock him up." But there are bubbles in Italian blood. When you scratch it you are liable to get an effervescent reaction . . . And at the finish both were roundly applauded. There were enough red bubbles in that hall to make a pudding that would reach to Mars . . . After the meeting I learned that on the night before 6000 preventative leaflets had been placed in the mail boxes of as many citizens by the members of this group . . . What an invigorating sight it would be could we but see our native drudges take heart and emulate these dark-skinned defiers . . .'

from The Journals of Herbert Minderman:

We continue our in-jail meetings of the Local 66. Spirits remain high and the sheriff responded by sending the guards to confiscate reading materials and tobacco. He has also taken away our regular food rations. Now it's down to bread and water twice a day. In response we have planned another battleship for lights-out tonight. My term is coming to an end. This afternoon I was taken from the cell and beaten on the legs. This seems to be a common treatment for any prisoner who has served his sentence. They said it was a warning. If I returned to the soapbox, next time I might not get out of jail alive. But fewer Wobblies are getting into the city because of vigilantes. Our supper was one cup of water and one piece of hard dark bread. One brother remarked that a battleship is better fueled on an empty stomach. When the men talk of loved ones and family, it's easy to grow sad. But I could not face my family if I ran from this fight.

Open Letter From Errico Malatesta
Translation by Rossa Nero

Anarchists have forgotten their principles. I would never have believed it possible that Socialists – even Social Democrats – would applaud and voluntarily take part, either on the side of the Germans or on that of the Allies, in a war like the one that is at present devastating Europe. But what is there to say when the same is done by Anarchists – not numerous, it is true, but having amongst them comrades whom we love and respect most?

I am not a pacifist. I fight, as we all do, for the triumph of peace and of fraternity amongst all human beings. But what has the present war in common with human emancipation, which is our cause? It is possible that present events may have shown that national feelings are more alive, while feelings of international brotherhood are less rooted than we thought. But this should be one more reason for intensifying, not abandoning, our anti-patriotic propaganda.

It is said that the victory of the Allies would be the end of militarism, the triumph of civilization and internatonal justice. The same is said on the side of the Germans. I have no greater confidence in the bloody Tsar, nor in the English diplomatists who oppress India, who betrayed Persia, who crushed the Boer Republics; nor in the French bourgeoisie, who massacred the natives of Morocco; nor in those of Belgium, who have allowed the Congo atrocities and have largely profited by them – and I can only recall some of their misdeeds, taken at random, not to mention what all governments and all capitalist classes do against the workers and rebels in their own countries.

Now as America is about to enter the war, I urge all American Socialists, especially the Anarchists, to do everything that can weaken the state and the capitalist class, and to take as the only guide to their conduct the interests of Socialism; or, if they are materially powerless to act efficaciously for their own cause, at least to refuse any voluntary help to the cause of the enemy, and stand aside to save at least their principles – which means to save the future.

– Errico Malatesta
London, England

November 1917

Giulia watched the wagon's slow approach. Salvatore and Francesco left before first light to meet the grape man on the Worcester Road. Last year's grapes were inferior, and Salvatore never forgot. This year he swore he would give that Neapolitan a piece of his mind. The previous year's wine was bitter; each time Salvatore took his first sip of the day, he cursed the Neapolitan and his bad grapes.

She finished her morning house chores and went out to uncover the press in the shed. Salvatore would want to do the first pressing when he arrived home. Since he heard Carlo was returning, he'd grown sullen. He was particularly annoyed that Giulia had killed two chickens and, when Carlo failed to appear, she had to cook the chickens before they went to waste. Salvatore ate them both down to the bones. But his communication with Giulia was now reduced to matters of function, and he refused to attend the wedding of the Polanskys' son.

She waved as the wagon approached. Francesco waved back with a smile. 'Good grapes this year,' bringing the horse to a halt.

'And that son-of-a-bitch Neapolitan knew it too. Never have I paid so much for a bushel of grapes. Giulia, some water for us.'

Giulia walked to the well and pumped water into the wooden bucket which she brought to the men, who gulped several tin cups-full. Then Francesco jumped on top of the wagon and began to hand Salvatore and Giulia straw baskets overflowing with sweaty blue-black clusters. When the wagon was half empty, they stopped for a count and determined that all of Salvatore's grapes were on the ground. Francesco said good-bye and in one motion sat on the wagon bench, picked up the reins, gave the two horses a holler and was off and running down the drive towards the road. Without a word Salvatore picked up baskets of grapes and carried them to the press.

For a few moments Giulia stood in silence watching the wagon. The breeze rustled strays of her gray pinned-up hair. The sun warmed her face and she looked up to it with eyes squinting in an attempt to absorb as much of the warm rays as possible. Despite facial lines and gray hair, she carried her youthful beauty. Her eyes were almond-shaped brown, her nose courtly and chin noble. A tall sturdy frame carried her as it did when she was in her teens, though now her bones ached at the end of the day and in the morning too. Turning, she caught a glare from Salvatore. He was waiting for her.

Before Giulia could grasp the press handle, Salvatore was dumping baskets of grapes. Within minutes she found the familiar rhythm of the rotation. When she was a young girl in Italy, she stomped the grapes, and stepping up and down in the large wooden barrel the grapes felt funny squishing under her bare feet. Later, something else stirred, and days later, stains and the smell of the fruit on her body made her tingly inside. Even as a boy, Luigi liked his wine and drank more than his fill. It was said that had he not been so drunk, the wagon would never have overturned.

One of the first things Salvatore did when he bought the farm was purchase the wine press at auction. A local farmer faulted on his loan and the bank auctioned everything. Carlo wanted to know where the family would go. Salvatore said that he did not know, but sometimes one man's loss was another man's gain. The smell of crushed grapes saturated the air. Bits of grape flesh and grape juice splattered Giulia's apron and face. She was turning the handle with both hands, lost in thoughts of Luigi, the death of her first-born Carolina, her disappointing years in America, Carlo, and how Salvatore's warm eyes once promised so much.

■ ■ ■

Vin's driving was treacherous. He ran red lights, stop signs, and cut people off. If I told him he just ran a stop sign he'd say, 'What do you want me to do, go back and stop?' If I reminded him that he'd just cut someone off he'd say, 'They're only going to the red light, when we were doing the same.' He ran cars off the road to make illegal turns, and, more than once, angered motorists chased us attempting to pull Vin over and give him a good thrashing. I called him Mr Magoo; he only looked ahead when driving. I never saw him use his rear-view mirror or look to his left or right when turning or traversing an intersection; and he never used turn signals. He'd blame a traffic jam on girls who see ads for sports cars which they buy and don't know how to drive.

No matter how much space there was for him when parallel parking, Vin collided with bumpers of cars he was parking between. That's what bumpers were for and he always managed to park with one of his tires up on the sidewalk. He rarely parked legally, so he received numerous parking tickets and fought every one of them, often winning by wearing down his opposition. In the Somerville Parking Commission office he was well known and the Commission would prefer tearing Vin's tickets up than listen to his indefatigable arguments.

He drove an old Dodge Dart which was in complete disarray. Trim flapped, fenders were rusted, the body paint looked as if the car had been under salt water. The hood, trunk, doors and quarter panels were dented. Tires were bald, the engine wouldn't stay running, seats were torn and the broken driver seat leaned all the way back to the rear bench seat so Vin drove without back support, holding himself up by the steering wheel. Windows were smudged from his cigar smoking, and there was no heat or defrost – when he drove in the rain he wiped the condensation with his shirt or jacket sleeve. During the winter the windshield continually froze over and had to be scraped. The old Dodge wouldn't pass inspection but Vin managed to buy a sticker illegally.

The Dodge died. Vin spent several weeks without a car, lauding the merits of walking and mass transit. Then he bought a used Toyota. This car was clean, but within weeks rust spots appeared on the body, windows took on a smoky film and dents appeared one by one. The brakes failed immediately, and Vin drove for several weeks using only his gear shift lever and the emergency brake. But then he ran a red light and nearly hit an old woman who was crossing the street. A police officer witnessed the incident, pulled him over to write a citation and had the car towed. The Toyota constantly leaked power steering fluid and made an annoying grind whenever Vin turned the wheel. He never locked his car, though the back seat overflowed with books. No one steals books, he said. And no one ever did.

Vin never downshifted when he drove, so in the city the car continually chugged and jerked down the street at low speeds. He'd drive obliviously on, elaborating on his latest diatribe.

'The quality of human life is eroding all around us. Just look at food, how the quality of produce and fish and meat is inferior to what it used to be, and now they've got this aqua-culture and corporate farming, who knows what we're eating, it all tastes the same. You pass by these yuppie stores who advertise home-made pasta. In the old days, home-made pasta was made *in casa*. How can you call it home-made if it's made in a store? And it's not just food, it's everything. Christ, take a look at the clothing people wear now. Years ago the people who made clothes were real craftsmen. If you bought a pair of shoes they were made by a real shoemaker. If you bought a shirt it was made by a real shirt cutter. But all the old craftsmen are gone now. And look at these fluorescent colors that everyone is wearing. I can't stand it. They're an offense to my eyes. These people shouldn't be allowed to wear such horrific colors. There's no such things as standards any more. Everything and everyone is on overload. Try to find some original conversation. People just talk about money or last night's sitcom. Alas, instead of making productive use of this century's technology and science, the human race has turned things against itself. Well. It's the curse of modernization: as soon as the ideal is reached, humans must break it down and destroy it.'

December 1917, South-Central Massachusetts

Carlo Valdinoci walks along an old railroad bed. Noonday sun thaws newly fallen leaves. A muddy smell hangs in the air, and the sun's rays speckle tiny water mirrors on defrosting foliage. He sits upon a large rock beside a stream pool and eats a piece of dry bread. The bread is sweet to his tongue. He goes down on his knees at the pool, swishes brown, red and gold leaves, takes an icy long drink from his reflection, rinses his face and returns to his seat. His thoughts are on Tina.

They shared the month of November making love, eating meals and taking walks. Tina updated him at length about recent developments in the movement, and she took him to the new movie house in Davis Square where Carlo saw his first motion picture. He was amazed, though light from the screen irritated his eyes and he couldn't read the script because it was in English; but he laughed with everyone else because of faces and gestures of the actors. Afterward, he contested: a generation of opinions would soon be formed by films.

Before long their old arguments ensued. Tina supported organization and unions; Carlo opposed syndicalism. And there was Fillipo. Tina didn't have to tell Carlo, he scented it when he saw them together.

Through a thicket of pines a female deer walks toward the stream with a large buck in pursuit. The doe speeds to a trot then slows long enough for the buck to sniff her genitals and attempt to mount her. She bounds off across the stream to the opposite bank with the buck following her. Carlo is startled by a loud snort behind him and turns to see another large buck tearing the ground with its hooves, snorting and challenging the first buck who, sighting the rival, begins his own ritual of snorting and tearing.

The animals charge each other and meet head-on with a crack

in the middle of the stream. They back off, rear up and ram again, wrestling with horns locked while the doe stands on the top of a small rise watching. Finally the first buck yields and bounds off across the stream to turn and watch the second buck begin his own courting ritual, following the doe up the hill, sniffing her trail and genitals. The two deer disappear and the lone buck walks into the brush.

It's one week to Christmas Eve. His mother has always stood behind him and she deserves some peace in her life. He rises, brushes himself off and continues along the railroad bed. Fried eels, spaghetti with anchovies and garlic, stuffed peppers, baccala with potatoes, calamari, zeppole, wine.

Eight Thousand March In Opposition To The War

Members of the Central Labor Union and other Leftist Socialist Organizations marched through the streets of Boston last Sunday to demonstrate their unified opposition to the war. Eight thousand Italians, Jews, Poles, Lithuanians, Irish and Greeks walked side by side holding signs that read 'If this is a Popular War, Why Conscription?,' 'Who Stole Panama?,' 'Who Crushed Haiti?, and 'We Demand Peace.'

As the march neared the end of Commonwealth Avenue to rally on the Boston Common, marchers were attacked by locally stationed sailors and soldiers on orders from officers. The marchers attempted to band together to resist but were overrun by the military troops which according to one observer 'seemed to come from every direction'. Dozens of marchers were wounded trying to make it to the safety of the Common where they were met by a group of mounted Boston Police who lent further chaos to the matter by advancing into the crowds and wielding clubs.

As a result of last week's actions, local Post Office Departments have begun to take away mailing privileges of any newspapers and magazines that print anti-war articles. This paper, and publications like *The Masses* have been banned from the mails. Where is our freedom of speech?

President Wilson continues to argue that this is a war of Democracy vs. Dictatorship. This is not true as our allies the Russians are certainly more of a dictatorship than our enemies the Germans. And the British themselves continue with their dictatorship over Ireland and India. When our own nation prevents the word from reaching the people, how can we call this democracy?

Contrary to President

Wilson's claims, the war is not a fight for self-determination, nor for a man to have the right to his own destiny. This is the fight that our comrades are fighting right now in Russia. As I write, Socialists, Communists and Anarchists are making gains against the Tsarist regime on all fronts, and have effectively disabled Tsarist Russia from participating in the war. The tighter the Wilson administration turns the lid, the harder we must fight to break out. Workers of the world, continue to unite and find strength in solidarity and opposition to the war!

– Rossa Nero

The Notebooks

'. . . About 65,000 men declared themselves conscientious objectors and asked for noncombatant service . . . Three men who were jailed at Fort Riley, Kansas, for refusing to perform any military duties, combatant or noncombatant, were taken one by one into the corridor . . . a hemp rope slung over the railing of the upper tier was put about their necks, hoisting them off their feet until they were at the point of collapse. Meanwhile the officers punched them on their ankles and shins. They were then lowered and the rope was tied to their arms, and again they were hoisted off their feet. This time a garden hose was sprayed on their faces with a nozzle about six inches from them, until they collapsed completely . . .'

■ ■ ■

'I can't believe it. If you would have told me even a few years ago what this administration was going to get away with I would have thought it impossible. Any progress made for human services over the past century these sons-of-bitches are going to demolish in a few years. Now that Reagan has broken the air-traffic controllers' strike, it'll set a precedent for a systematic dismantling of all the major unions because the public believes unions are a bad thing. Alas, American workers have no sense of how the eight-hour work day came to be, or why weekends and holidays are days off with pay or why workers' compensation developed. People think unions are anachronistic. Within a generation all jobs will be in the hands of multinational corporations and good jobs will have been exported overseas. And when the jobs are gone, instead of looking to the government for satisfaction and answers, the workers will fight amongst themselves. And most of it, dear Gregorio, as you know, is a misunderstanding, or no understanding – I don't know which is worse – of *history*. The labor struggles aren't taught as a significant part of American history. Christ, even the students paying attention come out of an American history course viewing labor history the same way they view slavery, like it happened in the past and has since been cured. Same with Sacco and Vanzetti, they teach the case as an ugly wrong committed in the distant past that could never happen again. The idea that a union might be necessary for workers to have some kind of voice in their workplace no longer exists, and before long the workforce will be working more hours for less money. Now that the cold war is coming to an end, the social distribution of wealth is going to be the next great problem for us to face. And we live in a society that refuses to even acknowledge its own unequal class structure. Christ, everybody thinks they're middle class while the middle class is shrinking before our eyes. Teachers are afraid to talk about social class or class conflict. And the standard immigrant story they teach is always the rags-to-riches story. Let's face it, the rags-to-riches story is a fraction of one percent of all immigrant experiences. It's always progress, onward and upward, instead of real experience. History should be more than biographies of so-called great men and grand events. It should certainly be more than a narrative uninformed by higher principles. But what kind of history do we have handed down but one full of unanswered fundamental questions? Everything gets lost in compartmentalization and the immense bureaucracy of documented, accepted scholarship. No one wants to hear anything outside of that. Alas. And it's not just the unions they're dismantling. They're going for health care, as you know from Carol. And they're going for education too. They'll strip health care and education clean. Christ, with some of this legislation going through now they're going to be putting tens of thousand of mental patients out on the street. What are all the workers going to do when all the factories and mills have moved to Mexico and South America and Asia? Americans are just standing by taking all of this like pigeons being thrown crumbs. I can't believe it. I've never been a religious man, Gregorio, and I don't believe in an afterlife. But I do believe in present life informed by the past. Alas. People are worn down. They don't have the time or the energy to apply their faculties to the issues. Nobody has a real opinion. Christ, there was a time when you could walk down on soap boxer's row on the Boston Common and there would be a dozen people expressing their opinions. Sure, you got few quacks, but there were some intelligent, informed people saying things. Public speaking really meant something. And without electricity you had to be a real orator to capture attention. There was an art to speaking and the best of them gathered the largest crowds. Well, now, all you have to do is pull the plug on a microphone and you effectively stop a speech to a stadium full of people. Alas. Just try to get some satisfaction with the health care industry, or an insurance company, or the electric company or the telephone company. Christ, have you tried calling any one of these lately? You don't even get a human being on the other end you get goddamned recorded voices. Computerized voices. I can't stand it. When the voice goes, so goes the culture. Well, I called the water company the other day because my bill jumped twenty-five percent in one month and I couldn't understand why. I spent a whole morning trying to get a fucking human being to talk to. I finally gave up. How can you explain your specific situation to a fucking computerized voice? When the human voice goes, human civilization goes. And service – it gets worse while costs go up. That goddamned second phone line I had installed last year has never worked right. The first time they sent out the installer it was a woman and when I asked her how long she'd been on the job she said she'd just started that year. I should have known then I was in for trouble. Three times since I've had service people out because every few days the line just goes dead. Every time a serviceman comes out they pick up the phone, get a dial tone and tell me there's nothing wrong with the phone. I try to explain that it doesn't happen all the time, could they rewire it or something, and they tell me that there's nothing they can do if it's working and I should call a supervisor. But try to get a goddamned supervisor from the telephone company on the telephone. You could call the president easier.'

Diary of Christina Donato:

'The Post Office takes away our mailing privileges. As a result, we distribute underground. When a new edition of The Watchdog *is ready, within days it is in the hands of readers through a system we have contrived whereby dozens of comrades pick up the publications at various locations and deliver them to union offices, factories, mills and taverns throughout the area. The same tactics are being used by others around the country. In addition to saving the movement money for postage, the new distribution system allows publications to reach readers faster and without interference. The government cannot keep the word from reaching the people. Fillipo is afraid the police may be watching us since Carlo is staying in my room. But he is wildly jealous. For all the police know Carlo fled to South America with the other Italians who left Mexico. I am more concerned that they are watching our operation through an informer. Antonio I would trust with my life, despite his greedy nature; but Ricardo is the kind of person who cannot look me in the eyes. I have long suspected that he holds out on us. I tell this to Fillipo, who says we must prove before we accuse.'*

The Memoirs of Errico Malatesta, Early Years

Abandoned by my comrades, I return to the Castello to bury the cases of rifles. I dig the entire afternoon in the rocky soil. It is disheartening that five cases of new carbines should be buried while in other parts of Italy hundreds of insurrectionists are without arms.

My part of the southern insurrection failed. But Giuseppe Mazzini proved that continued spontaneous popular uprisings, small and ineffective as they might be, are instrumental in slowly eroding the dominant system. We are a handful. But all progress and revolution has been the work of minorities.

Inside the Castello I eat bread, cheese, and drink wine. To the north-east, my long-time friends Andrea Costa and Carlo Cafiero are continuing with the insurrection. Tomorrow I rise early and find them. I fear that a river of blood separates the present from the future.

In my youth I studied rhetoric, Roman History and Gioberti's philosophy. My teachers did not succeed in stifling in me the forces of nature, so that I was able to preserve in the stupid and corrupting environment of a modern school my intellectual sanity and the purity of my heart.

When I was in Jesuit school, at fourteen, inspired by Mazzini and Garibaldi, I applied for membership to the Universal Republican Alliance. Mazzini refused my application because he thought my leanings were too socialistic and that I would eventually go over to the International. At that time, I had never heard of the International; but my curiosity was aroused and I took up the task to find out more and as a consequence I soon met Fanelli and Palladino.

When I wrote a letter to King Victor Emmanuel II and complained about social injustices, I was immediately arrested. Through my father's efforts I was freed, but my father warned that if I continued along the track I was following, I would find myself on the end of a rope. Later, I was expelled from medical school for taking part in a republican demonstration.

Then I met Bakunin and nothing was the same. It was during those inspiring months after the Paris Commune. I joined the International, ready for any sacrifice for the cause, inspired by the rosiest hopes. Cafiero and I went to Switzerland. I was sick spitting blood; it was said that I had consumption. While crossing the Gothard during the night (at that time there was no tunnel and one had to cross the snowy mountain in a diligence) I had caught a cold, and arrived at a house where Bakunin was staying in Zurich.

After our first greeting, Bakunin made up a camp bed, and invited me – he almost forced me – to lie on it, covered me with all the blankets he could lay his hands on and urged me to stay there quietly and sleep. And all this was accompanied by attention, and motherly tenderness, which gripped my heart.

While I was wrapped up in bed, and all present imagined that I was sleeping, I heard Bakunin whispering nice things about me and then adding sadly: 'What a shame that he should be so sick; we shall lose him very soon; he won't last more than six months.'

My dear friend Bakunin. Fifty years in his grave. But, his spirit and energy is the ink in my pen.

from The Journals of Herbert Minderman:

We put on a battleship through the night. Several times the guards came in and pounded the cell bars with their sticks. We jeered at them. By morning we grew tired and called off the battleship so we could rest. I lost my voice yelling. There was no breakfast. Around eight o'clock, firemen came to the jail cells and sprayed us with a high-power hose. We tried to build a mattress barricade but the water pressure swept the mattresses away and we were thrown against the cell wall. Some of the men got down flat on the floor but the firemen turned the hose down and the men were tossed like shrubs in a windstorm. Men collided in the air and when the firemen left, our clothes were shredded and our bodies black-and-blue. The cells were left under water and we are soaked and shivering in the December chill. Our calls for help go unanswered. A few of the men have broken, and when they are released they will give it up and go home.

■ ■ ■

Things began to unravel between Carol and me the summer before the October stockmarket crash. Carol was lobbying for us to marry although she knew I was opposed to the idea. It shouldn't be written in stone she said, we might at least allow a debate. Carol wanted to be a mother. I felt no desire to be a father and I abhorred the institution of marriage.

We'd been living together for nearly ten years and our relationship was fine. Sex relations slowed down but for us it was quality over quantity. We no longer went out on the club scene, except for an occasional jazz show. The commercialization of punk through new wave, the advent of CDs, had curtailed our interests in rock music. Grudgingly, I purchased a CD player. Then I purchased cassettes by the case, and as the Public Library expanded its CD library I borrowed discs and recorded new releases for pennies, and in that process I found something human amid the sterility of CDs. There was something intimate in making the tapes, adjusting the equalizer to my own specs, listing the songs, recording dates and players by hand.

It was easy being with Carol. She asked little of me and I was loved and trusted. We had our differences, especially on political matters. Carol was a pure democrat – a reformer, she believed in the potential of American democracy. I was afraid of the future; she wanted a hand in it. In terms of marrying, we might have continued our disagreement indefinitely had it not been for certain events.

Local neighborhoods were gentrifying one by one. Storefronts received facelifts, driveways that once parked used Fords yielded to new BMWs, Davis Square, with its new public transportation station, fell storefront by storefront. The little Greek breakfast joint was a juice and roll-up sandwich bar. They reopened and remolded the old theater which featured hip movies filling the void left by the defunct Orson Welles Theater in Harvard Square, which was now a Mexican restaurant chain. Mullens, an old neighborhood bar regularly full by 8.00 A.M., became an Irish Pub with live music serving international food. Americo's Shoe Repair was Bread and Butter, a gourmet take-out and catering service. They leveled the Day Street Bowling Alley for a new mall and it was rumored that a linen-tablecloth restaurant was going in next to the Rosebud Bar. When the wooden tenement across the street from us was sold, the Hispanic families moved out and during the summer the building went through a complete overhaul. Later, Sunday morning tours were attended by well-dressed, wide-eyed young couples who purchased over-priced apartments they wouldn't have considered renting two years previous.

One morning there was a knock on our door and a slick young man who drove an old Mercedes convertible introduced himself as our new landlord. Jim Calhoun informed us that he would begin renovating the building some time over the winter and thought we should get acquainted; he wanted to give us plenty of notice so we could find another living arrangement and at the same time offer us a ground-floor opportunity to purchase the apartment. I can't remember what the price, but I laughed in his face. Unmoved, he said when it went on the open market it would undoubtedly sell for ten thousand more. Carol and I should give the offer some serious consideration. After all, we were getting to that age where we had to start thinking about our future and financial security.

Right about that time Vin's mother died. He took it bad, especially since she was old and he had ample time to prepare himself. Her wake was attended by relatives, mostly old Italian women dressed in black who threw themselves on the coffin screaming, *Perche?*, and the men who gathered in corners speaking in Italian about the old days and how they only saw each other at funerals and weddings. I never saw Vin so shaken and disconcerted, and I remained by his side through several days of waking and the funeral. His brother was only present for short periods of time, antsy when he was there, making excuses for leaving.

For the next several weeks I expected Vin's condition to improve but it didn't. Whenever we talked, with tear-filled eyes he said he couldn't believe she was gone. He shipped her body to Italy to be buried alongside his father in a grave still unmarked. He visited various stone cutters to find one who satisfied him and settled on one of the Italians in Barre, Vermont. Then he spent several weeks making arrangements for himself and the monument to make the trip to Italy.

Carol and I had reached a critical point in our relationship. I didn't care about the new landlord, or our financial commitment to him. At the time, Carol had a good friend who was looking for a roommate. She had a place to go. Our marriage discussion had come to a head and burst, we were uneasy around each other.

Before Vin departed for Italy, we were having coffee. The stock market crashed the day before and the coffee shop was abuzz. Vin knew only sketchy details about the problems Carol and I were having. Since his loss and his scramble to get to Italy, I hadn't said much about what was happening in my life. He was unaware that our building had been sold. I told him that I thought my relationship with Carol was coming to an end, and he casually offered me a room in his house for as long as I needed.

Sheets of rain fell dark that afternoon as I walked drenched and chilled down Somerville Avenue, heart pounding from too many espressos and the thought of telling Carol I was leaving.

Christmas Eve, 1917

Giulia served both men second helpings of baccala and potatoes, and sliced several more thick slices of bread on the board between Carlo and Salvatore. Carlo reached for the wine and refilled his glass under Salvatore's cold stare. The meal was eaten in silence, as were others since Carlo's return. During that time Salvatore and Carlo said little to each other; Carlo was careful not to appear in the kitchen until Salvatore left for work in the morning; after dinner, Carlo took a walk and retired early to his room. He was constantly hungry, ate voraciously and slept twelve hours per night.

At a loss without anything to read or anyone to talk with besides Giulia, Carlo longed for Tina. The idea of her with Fillipo filled him with rage. Italy had entered the war. There was nowhere for him to go, no course of action he could see clear to take. His long-time friend Luigi Galleani was hiding out in Vermont. He wanted to return to see Tina first. It was only a matter of time before *The Watchdog* would be silenced. Her small firm body and birthmark on her forehead. Their recent time together had reawakened all of his passion for her.

'Merry Christmas,' Giulia said, raising a glass of water.

'Merry Christmas,' Carlo responded, raising his wine-filled glass. 'Delicious.'

Salvatore half-raised his glass, 'An atheist wishing us a Merry Christmas.'

There was quiet. For days the two men had walked around each other like animals of prey around a kill. Several nights after Carlo's arrival they argued and Salvatore said he would notify the authorities were it not for Giulia. Carlo's anarchism was childish and nothing but nonsense. Without government what would prevent people from doing whatever they pleased? Utter chaos would break out and society's weak would suffer far more than they already had. Salvatore insisted that if he was younger, he would gladly enlist and defend America and Carlo was gutless.

'It was your kind who caused all the trouble in Italy in 1897.'

'People were starving in Italy in 1897. You were one of the lucky ones who had a business to sell. What did you do but turn and run?'

'What do you know about Italy in 1897, you were only seven years old? The worst thing that happened to you was believing everything you read in those books. You became this anarchist from false ideals you learned in books.'

'No. I became an anarchist the first time you struck me when I was a boy. You know nothing of anarchism except for the misrepresentations the masters and their press have taught.'

In 1907, unable to get along with Salvatore, Carlo was sent back to Italy where he lived for five years with his uncle and aunt in Naples. Salvatore was glad to be rid of him, though Giulia protested. But the move backfired on Salvatore. In Italy, Carlo learned about Garibaldi, Mazzini, Errico Malatesta and Bakunin from his uncle who, unbeknownst to Salvatore, had joined the International. Living with his uncle in Naples, Carlo met many of the leading radicals of the day and attended anarchist conferences, read pamphlets, radical newspapers and other literature.

Carlo heard Errico Malatesta speak at a rally and was instantly struck by his convincing qualities and intelligence. Malatesta proposed to draw together all factions of the party and undermine the basis of the state. He advocated hindering the state's workings, paralyzing its services and unlimited propaganda until the occasion will one day arrive and the existing state could be overturned. As a boy, Carlo saw first hand how peasants in the countryside suffered during the winter and landlords never wanted for anything. In the cities factories and mills exploited workers and the owners reaped all the benefits. Though he later would oppose Malatesta's anarcho-syndicalism, during the Malatesta speech Carlo's life work became clear to him.

When Giulia first saw Carlo standing in the doorway she was horrified. He was thin, dirty, and appeared ten years older even though it had been less than two years since he went to Mexico.

His hair was graying, and dark lines circled his eyes. During the day Carlo helped her with the chores and they took meals together. Carlo told her what he'd seen in Mexico, and tried to convince her that his work was important enough to pursue, even if it meant imprisonment or deportation. Giulia could only see the boy at three years old who cried himself to sleep after Luigi died. Giulia married Salvatore because she wanted a father for Carlo, and agreed to move to America because she believed it to be in the best interest for all. Families were starving. She watched her daughter die and in her heart she knew Carlo was right; but she feared that his ideals would spell his end.

The Memoirs of Errico Malatesta, Early Years

Chest ailments, of the same type that claimed my mother, brother and sister, killed my father. I handed over the modest amount of property that I inherited to the tenants. What money came to me I put into propaganda. There was no going back.

But I was faced with the problem of how to earn a living, so I began to learn the mechanics trade, working, and living, among the people. I knew from the beginning if I was going to make revolution, I must live among the people.

Bakunin is my spiritual father, though I find his dictatorial views of authority and state too Marxian. But he is a force in the new anarchist movement in Italy. He has been integral in provoking organized strikes, demonstrations, restoring our Mazzinian and Garibaldian tradition of the insurrection.

It is not simply a matter of emancipating the people, but the people must be inspired to emancipate themselves. A new way of life must emerge from the body of the people themselves, and correspond to the state of their development and advance as they advance.

I believe that workers must find in union the moral, economic, and physical strength needed to subdue the organized might of the oppressors. The workers cannot arrive at anarchism in one leap. He must learn to co-operate with others in defense of common interests, and by struggling against the bosses, and government which supports oppression, realize that bosses and governments are useless parasites and that the workers can manage by their own efforts.

My father always told me that no one person can change the world, or the course of history. He was a man of moderation and middle ground. But each man must choose his own line of conduct.

Bolsheviks Seize Power Pledge Socialist Future

The Bolshevik faction of the Russian Revolutionary movement seized power in Russia last month. This marks for the first time in Russian history a secular government. The Bolsheviks have promised a socialist future in Russia, one that will consist of a technologically advanced collective society.

The Bolsheviks pledge a rapid industrialization and a rapid democratization. The call is for a political revolution as means to produce a new political subject, to perceive and act upon its class interests in a collective way.

While the United States and its propagating press continue to criticize and distort the revolution in Russia, socialists around the world, and in the United States, should support the Bolshevik movement regardless of its supposed shortcomings. As U.S. troops steam across the Atlantic Ocean to fight the capitalist war, now is the time for revolutionaries to remain united in the fight for freedom, and opposition to the war in Europe.

In what country is freedom of speech blocked? Where are labor disputes won by government and industry-backed force which supports machine-gunning miners striking for decent working conditions? Where are immigrants being jailed and deported? Where are labor activists tried, convicted and even executed on false charges? Where are citizens being called upon to turn in to authorities the name any one they suspect of being seditious? Where is conscription being forced upon unwilling men to fight and die in an unfair war? Where are men being lynched without government interference just because of the color of their skin?

The dictatorship is not in Tsarist Russia, but under Tsar Wilson and his henchman Attorney General Palmer. Now is not the time to criticize the flaws in the Russian Revolution. We must stand together and extend the struggle on our own soil while we still have the legs under us.

– Rossa Nero

Diary of Christina Donato:

'On Christmas Eve we strike gold. Fillipo borrows an automobile and we drive to a suburb south of Boston where many factory owners and bosses live. Fillipo has previously cased the town, and we park the auto on a back woods road then walk a trail which leads to a street lined with large red brick homes, and sneak unnoticed through backyards, trying to find a home that is not occupied. We thread our way down one end of the street, cross at the dead end out of sight, and sneak down the other side. The homes we pass are alive with voices and music and large groups of people drinking, eating and laughing. Inside the second-to-last house on the street, only one night light is lit on the first floor. The second floor is dark. There are no autos in the carriage house and by all appearances the house is empty. The four of us make our way around the house looking for a window to climb in. Fillipo tries the back door and it is unlocked. We hear more laughter from some distant warm living room. The celebrations will distract the neighbors and prevent them from detecting our presence. We spread out, and I climb a grand staircase to the second floor into a long hallway. It is dark but the full moon allows enough light through the large windows so that I can see. The first room off the hallway is a nursery. Next is an older child's room. The third is a guest room; inside is an empty bed, dresser and night table. Across the hall is the master bedroom containing a woman's dressing table with an open jewelry box overflowing with earrings, bracelets, necklaces and brooches. I gather everything in sight and place it into my bag. The bench in front of the dressing table is padded, and I sit looking around the room. Objects take shape out of the darkness. A large canopy bed. Night tables on each side of the bed. A cushioned chair in one corner. A second in the other corner. There is a dresser as wide as it is tall the size of the wall, floor to ceiling. I turn and in the dressing mirror my reflection startles me.

I stare into the mirror at my face in the moon light, rubbing my dry cheeks above the creams, makeup, powders, brushes and combs that line the top of the table. I sweep them into my bag. Fillipo calls and running for the stairs I trip over a chair in the hall. I call for Fillipo who climbs the stairs and helps me to my feet and down to the first floor where Ricardo and Antonio are excited. This is the best haul ever. We leave through the back door past houses full of unaware holiday celebrators. I am unable to walk on my right ankle so Antonio takes my bag and I throw my arm around Fillipo. Antonio and Ricardo run ahead, urging us to hurry so that we can get out of town before we are discovered. In my room, hardly a square inch of the floor is free with all the silverware, crystal, jewelry. Ricardo and Antonio sit at the kitchen table opening the wrapped gifts of a gold watch, jeweled necklace, expensive dolls, mechanical toys and a fur coat. Fillipo says we cannot take the loot to the fence all at once, but over time. If we bring it all at once he'll never pay us what it is worth. Besides, it is too risky since there is sure to be something about the robbery in the newspapers. If the family is important enough, the police will squeeze the local pawnshops and fences. We can't trust the Irishman. We will have to find a new fence. Antonio and Ricardo insist that since it is Christmas, we are entitled to keep some of the loot for ourselves. Ricardo wants one pair of earrings for his girlfriend and Fillipo says no. My ankle is swollen and Fillipo is down on the floor examining it. He says it is sprained.'

The Notebooks

'... If a worker loses his life, are his dependents compensated in any way? In some cases they are and in some cases not. If he is crippled for life is there any compensation? No, sir, there is none . . . Then the whole burden is thrown directly upon their shoulders? Yes, sir. The industry bears none of it? No, the industry bears none of it . . . The well-paid leaders of the AFL were protected from criticism by tightly controlled meetings and by "goon" squads – hired toughs originally used against strikebreakers but after a while used to intimidate and beat up opponents inside the union . . . We are here to confederate the workers of this country into a working-class movement that shall have for its purpose the emancipation of the working class from the slave bondage of capitalism . . . The aims and objects of this organization shall be to put the working class in possession of the economic power, the means of life, in control of the machinery of production and distribution, without regards to the capitalist masters . . . The working class and the employing class have nothing in common. There can be no peace so long as hunger and want are found among millions of working people and the few, who make up the employing class, have all the good things of life . . . Between these two classes a struggle must go on until all the toilers come together on the political as well as on the industrial field, and take hold that which they produce by their labor, through an economic organization of the working class without any political party . . .'

The Memoirs of Errico Malatesta, Early Years

Smoke swirls up and is carried by the wind. Andrea Costa, Carlo Cafiero and I assure the villagers they have nothing to fear. We call for an end to the reign of King Victor Emmanuel, and encourage the people to put out their landlords.

Several insurgents return with more tax registers and toss them into the fire. The villagers are uneasy. I plead with them to listen to me.

I tell them there exists no natural law which determines what part of the peasant's earnings should go to him. And if such a law did exist, those earnings could not be less than what is needed to maintain life. The oppression which impinges directly on those who work the land and causes their children's hunger-pains during winter is the economic oppression forced on them by the landlords who subject them to such exploitation. To destroy this oppression without any danger of it re-emerging, you must believe that you have a right to a fair share of your own productivity. You must exercise your basic right by expropriating the land owners and putting their wealth at the disposal of your own people. You must learn to establish yourselves into associations and organize production on your own terms. You are the ones who have the ability and the technical skills to do so, not the landlords who could do nothing without you. Harvest everything and give nothing to them! They are strong because they have made laws to legitimize their situation. They have organized a system of repression to defend themselves from your demands under the name of property and commerce. They have made it so they will call you thief when you try to take what is rightfully yours. They are the robbers. You must deprive the present holders of their power and wealth by putting the land and means of production into your own hands. Do not fear that the dispossessed landlord will hire soldiers to restore order. Dispossess them completely and they will find that without money they can employ no one.

The villagers lose interest. The burning tax registers reduce to a pile of smoldering ashes and the priest reminds us that these are simple people; while the villagers are sympathetic to what we say, what we propose is impossible for them imagine or act upon. They know what happens when men begin to take the kind of measures that we suggest. If the landlords put them out they will have nowhere to go. It is easy for outsiders who can read and write and talk eloquently, to come here and expect these people to follow them into the unknown.

A watch posted on a nearby hilltop signals that a troop of soldiers approaches from the south-west. The priest instructs us to take the north-east road. Once in the hills, we will be able to disperse.

In the foothills we bury our weapons and go separate ways. I walk north for the remainder of the afternoon, and remain outside the perimeters of the villages that mark the countryside. As it begins to darken I turn west towards Naples.

■ ■ ■

I never loved her as I did those few days between breaking the news and going. I took much about her for granted and suddenly I noticed everything new. Her delicate frame, those thin legs and tiny ankles, her small firm breasts, shapely ass, high cheekbones, smooth dark skin, perfect mouth, button nose which I teased seemed strange for a Greek. Her eyes were oversized brown and she kept her shiny black hair short in a funky cut. Nonetheless I packed up my things, paid her my share of the rent due, and the afternoon I was going to leave she tearfully said she couldn't bear to watch me go so she went out to a movie by herself and I believe she was hoping I would be there when she returned.

I've never figured out how I left her nor met her equal. Something was missing inside me and I felt like an impostor, believing somehow that any time I might be exposed as someone not worthy of such respect and intimacy. I never saw her after that. Once I received a postcard after she moved to San Francisco, found a publisher for her first book of poetry, and was falling in love with an architect. I left her like running an errand.

Vin departed for Italy the day after I moved in so I had his place to myself. Every day I thought to call Carol and ask her if I could move back. I had the creeps sleeping in Vin's mother's bed, she died so recently during her sleep. But soon I was comfortable enough on the high hard mattress and box spring under the oversized crucifix hanging over the large mahogany headboard.

Vin's house was decomposing from the outside-in. Roof shingles rotted off, sideboard shingles cracked and fell, red paint browned. White paint on window frames and porch pillars grayed and peeled. Porch stairs and porch boards were broken and warped, wrought iron railings rusted. Bushes and hedges grew untrimmed, weeds stood up through holes in what was once a hot-top driveway. Inside an overriding smell of cigars dominated the place, windows were dirty, white window shades yellow and torn. Long irregular cracks lined the ceilings and walls, bookshelves overflowed on to the floor and books and magazines stacked half way to the ceiling. Vin was a music lover. One of his dictums was that he could never like anyone who didn't like Bach and he had hundreds of Bach albums.

The kitchen was unorganized and dirty, the stove in particular needed cleaning. The dining room was laden with books, records and papers. It was also the home of Vin's coveted liquor cabinet. Vin loved to drink and hardly a week passed without one of his friends or 'contacts' from France, or Italy, or Spain coming to town with some kind of local brandy, sherry or grappa. Vin was especially fond of grappa and his cabinet contained dozens of varieties.

The study was off the side of the dining room and filled with mountains of books, file cases stacked on file cases. Both of the room's windows were blocked with book cases and there was barely room for Vin's desk, chair, computer and micro-film machine.

I spent those first two weeks browsing the stacks and bookshelves of Vin's library which contained poetry, music, history, politics, anarchism, philosophy, biography, novels, drama, science and the visual arts. His records and tapes consisted of jazz and classical, with emphasis on opera. I played records, read excerpts from books and drank Vin's liquor, feeling sorry for myself, thinking about Carol and growing angry at her for not fighting harder to keep me from leaving.

from The Journals of Herbert Minderman:

Two days ago I was released. My father and mother were horrified at the sight of me. I lost some weight and there are bruises on my face. Mom cooked chicken, potatoes and corn and I ate till it felt like I would burst. My family wanted to know what it was like in jail. I told them all about our battleships and the firemen with the hoses. But I didn't tell them about the beatings because I didn't want to put the fright into my mother. But my father knows full well, and after supper he took me for a walk and pleaded with me not to return to the soapbox. He fears for my life and says that I did my good part, no one can say otherwise. If I keep out of trouble he can find me a postal service job with him. But I told him there was still a fight. Without free speech there was no free country. It was his proper raising me that leaves me no choice. I write under oil lamp, my younger brothers asleep in their bunks. I do not fear tomorrow. It sure is good to have my belly full and a warm bed. But men are hungry and cold in jail. Some day if anyone reads these words, everything I write is true.

January 1918

Giulia waved and watched Carlo lift his collar and disappear into the woods. Snow swirled in a gusty wind. She pleaded with Carlo to remain until the storm was over. Salvatore wanted him out. Giulia gave Carlo twelve dollars, all the money she had.

As he walked off into the storm, Giulia recognized the fear she'd known since Carlo was sixteen and left home for Italy. Each year that Carlo grew older he seemed to be deeper in trouble. She wondered what would have happened if she'd stayed in Italy. Salvatore was a good man; but she never loved him, not the way she loved Luigi. Whenever she looked at Carlo now she could see Luigi and his short broad frame, mustache, crooked teeth and olive green eyes. In the early days Salvatore and Carlo got along well and little Carlo accompanied Salvatore with his fish cart and over supper Carlo excitedly reported the day's events. But as Carlo grew older something came between them, and Giulia found herself in the middle trying to appease both sides. Salvatore began to resent Giulia, he told her she was going to ruin Carlo if she treated him like a baby. Things grew worse in America, and Salvatore hit Carlo. Carlo fought back. By the time he was fifteen his body was developing and once he and Salvatore beat each other bloody during the harvest. Not long after the incident Salvatore suggested that Carlo be sent back to Italy, it would be good for him and he could learn a trade. The next time Carlo and Salvatore got into a brawl, Giulia agreed.

Salvatore's plan was to have Carlo return to Italy and learn shoe-making from Salvatore's brother-in-law. In a few years Carlo would return to help out on the farm and work his trade in the nearby towns. But Carlo only returned to America at the urging of his new associates in Italy who assured him he could help perpetuate the struggle in the United States. Much to Salvatore and Giulia's horror, when Carlo finally came back, he was professing himself to be a revolutionary. Salvatore burned all the books and pamphlets that Carlo brought with him from Italy, and told him that it was his home and as long as Carlo lived under his roof he would live under his rules. Carlo moved to New York City.

Giulia flashed to an incident that occurred when she was a little girl and the men came to her village and caused a disturbance. She remembered the small man with red hair and beard who lifted her into the air speaking words she did not understand. When Carlo first returned from Italy with his literature, she recognized the man who lifted her as the man in a newspaper photo. She asked Carlo who the man was, and he said it was Errico Malatesta, the great revolutionary leader. She was shivering and didn't know how long she was standing outside. Her clothes were wet and icy water seeped down her neck.

Government Cannot Meet The Needs of the People

The idea of a representative democracy can only mean a passive citizenship. A citizen may be free when he votes, but after that he is reduced to a subject who is too resigned to entertain higher expectations of society. Americans are only free during the electing of their leaders. After the leaders are elected officials only serve the interests of the minority élite.

Government has shown time and again, that it is a puppet in the hands of big business. What good can votes do when most of the wealth, power, property and industry is in the hands of the tiniest minority of the country's population? Has the vote helped to free the poor and downtrodden from injustice? Has the vote prevented the lynching of Negroes in the south, or the machine-gunning of striking workers? Has the vote stopped our nation from sending innocent, poor young men to early deaths for wars that line the pockets of the rich? Has the vote ended the beating and jailing of citizens demanding their right to free speech?

Workers: The best government is no government. The vote is the biggest lie in this democracy. The people cannot count on the national government. Take control over your own life: it is in your hands. Voting can only further the stranglehold the government has on your throats.

– Rossa Nero

The Notebooks

'. . . The history of the political activities of man proves that they have given him absolutely nothing that he could not have achieved in a more direct, less costly, and more lasting manner. As a matter of fact, every inch of ground he has gained has been through a constant fight, a ceaseless struggle for self-assertion, and not through suffrage. There is no reason whatever to assume that woman, in her climb to emancipation, has been, or will be, helped by the ballot . . . Her development, her freedom, her independence, must come from and through herself. First, by asserting herself as a personality. Second, by refusing the right to anyone over her body; by refusing to bear children, unless she wants them; by refusing to be a servant to God, the State, society, the husband, the family, etc., by making her life simpler, but deeper and richer . . . Only that, and not the ballot, will set woman free . . .'

The Memoirs of Errico Malatesta, Early Years

A fat bald priest with a dent in his forehead instructs me to follow him. The hills are swarming with police and soldiers; the priest has discovered me hiding amongst barrels in the barn behind the church. Many of the clergy members have been sympathetic towards the insurrectionists; however, they caution us that our efforts to move the people to action are likely to be futile.

The priest opens the barn door and looks in both directions. He waves for me to follow him and we rush to the entrance of the church where he opens the heavy door and pushes me in.

The inside of the church is ablaze with tiers and tiers of burning candles. The scent of melting wax fills the air, and light from a thousand flames forms a red, yellow, and orange wave. A massive marble altar is strewn with gold candleholders, and a gold communion cup overflows with wine.

I follow the priest down a narrow hallway sparsely lit with candles. The vestibule smells strongly of incense, and at one of the vestibule walls the priest opens a trick door and motions for me to follow him down a spiraling set of creaking wooden stairs into a dimly lit room, which leads to another hidden doorway. We pass and enter another room, in which there is a large desk and chair with oversize leather bound books sitting on the desk.

I can hear choral singing as we pass through yet another door into a chamber with wooden boxes stacked in the shadows. We proceed down a dark corridor into a square room with yellow walls, each lit with one candle in one holder. Except for a wooden chest on the far end against the wall, the room is empty. The chest is made of walnut, inlaid with wood and stucco. A coat of arms and classical vases with overflowing flowers are carved into three separate front panels.

The priest opens the lid of the chest. He says that I will be safe. I climb inside the chest which allows only enough room for me to stretch my legs. He closes the lid and everything goes black. A door slams shut and the sound of a key turns in the blind silence.

I lay in the chest for an undetermined amount of time, hungry, my body aching. I smell walnut, incense, melting wax and wine. I try to push the lid up but it is sealed shut. I kick and shout and the sound of choral singing grows louder. I try one more time to get out, pushing my hands and knees with all of my strength on the lid which bursts open.

Bright sun and blue sky. My heart beats heavily. My lungs are congested and I am short of breath. The heavy old man driving the hay wagon tells me to stay down because police are in the area.

I sleep and wake to the clip-clop of horse hooves. The wagon comes to a stop and I sit up to look upon the Bay of Naples.

■ ■ ■

Vin returned from Italy in better spirits. It was good his parents were settled where they belonged. Some of his mother's personal belongings were still in the dresser and Vin gave me a cardboard box and asked me to bring them down to the basement.

Those first weeks Vin was back we took long breakfasts of biscotti and several pots of espresso laced with anisette. Breakfast slid into lunch. Vin liked the idea of my food foraging, but he turned his nose up to eating anything I brought from work, though he did drink the wine. Each day we walked to La Cascia's for a fresh loaf of good bread – Vin insisted he would never live in a neighborhood where he couldn't get good bread – sliced proscuitto, a wedge of provolone, olives, and then return to Vin's and listen to Bach, opera, scratchy old Lester Young and Ben Webster albums until mid-afternoon when Vin brewed more espresso we laced with anisette and smoked Vin's cigarillos while Vin mocked Webster's windy sound, pretending to blow a sax, or sat back humming Bach air conducting. Too bad your ears have been polluted by rock and roll he said. He hated rock 'n' roll, hated all electric music which he claimed made you deaf. If I attempted to defend rock 'n' roll, Vin would head me off. Gregorio, Gregorio, there are only two kinds of music. There's good music, and there's bad music. Vin never heard any rock 'n' roll that he could call good music. If anything, rock 'n' roll was theater. And even that, he said, was questionable.

Late afternoons we took another walk to buy a piece of veal, pasta and salad makings, and cooked through evening, drinking beer and listening to music. Vin talked about his pecking order of hell and how number one on that list was self-consciousness and everyone was too hung up and afraid to have a good shit for themselves and we shouldn't politicize sex, the gays were wrong to be making sex a political issue because sex was pleasure not politics. He'd bemoan the education system and how political correctness and multi-culturalism were ruining education, what public education owed any student was to teach them the basics of reading, writing, math and science and the rest was up to the student. He was fond of talking about his own youth and his love for the old library and now with the new-fangled library with its ugly architecture they'd taken the humanness out of it. He began reading when he was five or six years old, falling in love with adventure books like *Treasure Island*. In the seventies the FBI bugged his phone. I asked him did he censor his calls and he said no. After all, on the other end of the line was some Ivy League dope in a trench coat, who knows, if the guy was listening he might learn something.

More wine. More food. More of Vin's talk about anarchism being in a state of suspension between the needs of an old era and the opening of a new. People were disempowered and didn't believe that the destiny of society lies within their hands. The human machine was running headlong out of control without any rational means to keep it in check. And all one had to do was look at the schools and the mass media to see that the spirit of rebellion had been effectively subverted.

Sometimes I thought Vin would go on talking and never stop. Then he'd brush his hair back with his hands, say an obligatory 'Alas,' and rise to clear the dinner dishes which he washed and I dried. Back into the dining room with a pot of espresso, more Bach, Charlie Parker, Serge Chaloff, select liqueurs, brandies and grappas from his cabinet, 'Try a little of this one, Try a little of that.' My head would spin. Late in the evening Vin wielded the deadliest of them all – the *Centa Herba*, some kind of green poison in a round bottle one hundred and thirty proof.

In the middle of a diatribe it might strike him that there was someone else in the room and he'd stop in mid-sentence.

'Have you talked to Carol recently?'

'No. But I should. Christ, I'm still not sure why I left her.'

'By the way,' he'd interrupt. 'Did I tell you I'm going up to Lawrence to visit old Joe Spanna next week? I told you about Joe, he's one of the last of the old-timers, veteran of the Lawrence strike, well, he and his wife – in fact she was with the first group of women who went out. Anyway, Joe's one of the last of the Italian anarchists from the turn of the century movement still alive in this country. As a matter of fact Valdinoci hid out in his attic for a while when he was on the run. He's in a nursing home, but sadly he's failing. Old Joe still has his pistols buried somewhere for when the insurrection comes, though the last time I talked with him he couldn't remember where he buried them.'

Vin poured me another healthy dose of *Centa Herba*. I took a swallow and dizzily swirled around in my chair. Vin shook his head in that twitchy lamentful shake of his.

'Alas, they don't make them like Old Joe any longer.'

January 1918

Half-way across the frozen Charles River the trolley shakes in a wind-gust. The golden State House dome's smothered by a white swirl shrouding Beacon Hill. Carlo Valdinoci bounces his half-frozen feet on the trolley floor.

At Harvard Station, end of the line, Carlo puts up his collar. He places his hands in his pockets, tucks his chin under the upper part of his coat and steps into the storm through Harvard Square, down Broadway to Columbia, a right on to Cambridge Street, down an unmarked alley, then he cuts through the backside of East Cambridge into the Somerville meat-packing district. The poor visibility confuses him and he walks down one small side street and up another before finding his bearings and the tavern.

It is smoky inside, crowded with workers, the smell of sawdust, beer, roasting meat and coffee permeates the air. A hand goes up from a wooden booth. Carlo hangs his coat on a hook next to the booth and slides on to the wooden bench opposite Tavenese, who reaches into his shirt pocket for a folded piece of paper and slides it across the table under his hand. Carlo takes the paper and unfolds it, Good Hope Road, Barre, Vermont. Carlo tears the paper into tiny pieces which he tosses onto the sawdust floor.

Carlo eats a sandwich while Tavanese speaks of an impending meat-packers' strike and, to Carlo's dismay, sings the praises of William Foster. The potential for a nation-wide strike will mean federal intervention and improved conditions. If the steel industry doesn't watch out they'll be Foster's next target. Carlo cannot believe what he hears from his old anarchist friend.

Snow wind-tunnels down the red brick plant-lined street. Carlo turns toward Union Square where he stops to look up at the new electric sign erected while he was in Mexico, barely visible in the snowfall: BOOST SOMERVILLE, DO YOUR SHOPPING AT HOME. He walks fuming down Somerville Avenue towards Tina's apartment, his thoughts fixed on Tavanese's words. *Anarchism has reached its end, there were no longer any great anarchist leaders in the movement. Socialism is the wave of the future, it is time to recognize that fact.*

Inside, Outside: An Urge for Re-Consideration

As the capitalist war rages in Europe, tens of thousands of young men die by the week. Now is the time to remind ourselves that while some of us are still on the outside, hundreds are incarcerated nationwide for doing nothing more than speaking freely in opposition to the war.

Kate Richards O'Hare is serving five years in the Missouri state penitentiary, for reportedly saying that 'the women of the United States were nothing more nor less than brood sows, to raise children to get into the army and to be made into fertilizer'.

In Boston the twenty-four men and women arrested last September have all been found guilty under the Espionage Act and given sentences ranging from one to twelve years.

In South Dakota a farmer named Fred Fairchild was sentenced to one year and a day at Leavenworth penitentiary. He was accused of claiming that if he were of conscription age, he would refuse to serve.

In Chicago, Charles Schenck's Supreme Court appeal was unanimously turned down and he will serve out the rest of his sentence.

The trial for the 165 I.W.W. leaders rounded up last September and still in prison, has been set for April.

Emma Goldman and Alexander Berkman are presently serving sentences for their anti-conscription activity.

For those of us on the outside, our continued unity and support is necessary if we are to put an end to such oppression. We mustn't let the government split our factions apart, despite our differences. Socialists, Wobblies, Anarchists, Communists, stand together as the masses have in Russia.

1918 is an election year. All over the nation the Socialist Party has candidates running on all levels. If we are presentably unable to effect revolutionary change from without, we must contemplate the nature of change from within. In the past, this very paper had published editorials in opposition to the vote. Perhaps at this time those eligible to vote should reconsider their options, and support the socialist ticket.

– Rossa Nero

The Notebooks

'... The most stringent protection of free speech would not protect a man in falsely shouting fire in a theatre and causing a panic ... The question in every case is whether the words used are used in such circumstances and are of such a nature as to create a clear and present danger that they will bring about the substantive evils that Congress has the right to prevent.'

■ ■ ■

Old Joe Spanna was a shell of a man, propped up in his nursing-home bed, a daft grin on his drooling mouth, skin white as bed sheets, chest sunken, arms wire-thin.

'Joe,' Mrs Spanna said. 'Look who is here.' Joe looked up at Vin, his head bobbing an endless bob, a grin widening into a smile that suggested he recognized Vin. Vin introduced Joe to me. I extended my hand to him but withdrew the gesture realizing it was futile. The three of us stood around the bed for several minutes in an awkward silence until Vin broke in with an alas.

A smell of urine permeated the air and Vin and Mrs Spanna exchanged talk about Joe's condition. She said that it didn't look good and it was hard for her to see him like this. All the while Joe looked up at us with his smile and head bobbing, white saliva drooling down his chin which Mrs Spanna wiped dutifully away with tissue. Best thing they could do for him now was keep him comfortable, and for several long minutes we exchanged niceties. Mrs Spanna invited us to her house for lunch then leaned over to kiss Joe on his forehead. Vin told him to keep up the struggle. I offered a slight wave and said nice to meet you. Joe smiled, his head bobbed.

We followed Mrs Spanna in her big old Pontiac. Until Joe's health began to fade a decade earlier, she was a full-time social activist arrested no less than a dozen times. During the seventies she wrote articles and helped with the paste-up work in Vin's magazine, and she still volunteered at a local shelter for homeless women. The daughter of Polish immigrants, she moved to Lawrence from her family's farm in southwestern Massachusetts when she was twelve. In Lawrence she lived with relatives and worked in a wool mill. Vin said it was hard to believe she was eighty-eight years old, and it was. She looked twenty years younger.

Her small white house was located on an unassuming street in a Hispanic neighborhood once home to immigrants from all over Europe. The latest wave came from South America, Puerto Rico, and Asia, though mills and factories were no longer in operation. The Spanna home was simple: furniture, drapes and wallpaper dulled and worn but the dwelling was immaculately clean. In the living room a large book case held hundreds of old leather bound books of leftist literature, fiction writers like Zola and Dickens, and hundreds of volumes in Italian. There was an ancient record player and a stack of 78s with decomposing cardboard covers. We sat around a small dining-room table and Mrs Spanna served us a delicious potato and leek soup with a hearty bread and beer. She drank water. Lunch talk was about the old days and people I'd never heard of and Vin lamented how things weren't like they used to be, and Mrs Spanna said that was true but in some ways they were better, there's always small ways in which things get better. Over her protests I helped her clear the plates and bring everything into the kitchen. She wouldn't allow me to wash; instead she told us to sit in the living room and she made coffee.

She was a tall lean woman with white hair streaked black. Her face was remarkably line-free for a woman of eighty-eight, with smoothly carved features, and she moved with the energy and agility of a woman half her age. She brought in a tray with a pot of coffee, cream, sugar and slices of home-made pound cake. We fixed ourselves coffee and took a slice of cake, each of us sitting at a different point in the living room. I choose the sofa, which had a worn mahogany cocktail table in front of it, Vin sat in an armchair by a window and Mrs Spanna settled into a wooden rocker with a cup of coffee on her lap, gently rocking. I wanted desperately to ask her about the Lawrence Strike, but I didn't know how. I looked over at Vin and could tell that he was getting ready to begin one of his monologues so before he got a word out of his mouth, I said, 'Mrs Spanna, tell me about the Bread and Roses Strike.'

She lifted herself upright in the rocker, delicately placed her coffee cup back on to its saucer and put it on the lamp table next to her chair. A quiet smile came over her face; maybe she had been expecting me to ask that question, or had been wishing that I would. She turned and looked me in the eye as if to size me up and assess whether I was worth the effort. There were a few seconds of silence.

'The strike. Well. That was a long time ago, of course. And I was just a girl, really. Children worked in the mills. I was twelve, and there were younger. Some died within two or three years. It was a woolen mill. I'd moved to Lawrence to live with relatives when things weren't working out on my parents' farm. There were two brothers but they were needed on the farm so my parents sent me to Lawrence. My aunt and uncle kept a little of my earnings for my keep and the rest of the money went to my parents at the farm. We lived in an over-crowded tenement building in one of the neighborhoods not far from here. There were Poles, Portuguese, French-Canadian, English, Irish, Russians, Italians, Syrians. We all lived in the neighborhoods and everybody, men, women and children, worked in the mills.

'I worked at a mill alongside other Polish women. Weavers. We worked long hours and some days I never saw daylight. Six days a week. The conditions were deplorable. Stairways were broken, what few windows were dirty and allowed in little or no light. In fact the only light I remember came from gas jets which burned night and day. The lavatory was filthy. There was no fresh drinking water and the building was infested with mice and roaches. In the winter we froze and in the summer we suffered from heat. Children worked alongside men and women. I'd been on the loom about a year, of course we were already earning dreadfully low wages, when suddenly, a few weeks after Christmas our wages were reduced. Just like that. We were told our wages were being reduced and if we didn't like it, there were plenty of people who would be willing to replace us. It's funny because whenever I think of that time, I don't recall how we ever found the nerve, but the women stopped the work on the looms and walked out. Just like that. Well, the next day, five thousand workers at another mill quit. They marched to another mill, rushed the gates and shut off the power, calling on the workers to walk out. Soon there were ten thousand workers out on strike.

'Of course we had no organization. Some of the workers in the know telegraphed Wobbly leader Joseph Ettor. He was in New York City and they asked him could he help us conduct the strike. Of course I'd heard of the Wobblies but at the time most of the strikers didn't belong to the I.W.W. But when Ettor arrived a committee of fifty was set up to represent all nationalities and interests. As I recall most of the committee was made up of Wobblies and they organized mass meetings, parades and soup kitchens. You see, by this time, fifty thousand workers were on strike and had to be fed. In fact, that's where I met Joe, in a soup kitchen where he came to eat. For the duration of the strike I worked in a soup kitchen seven days a week. Three meals a day. There were so many to be fed no sooner did we finish one meal we had to get ready for the next. Of course I heard of anarchists among the mill workers but Joe was the first one I ever personally knew. It scared me in the beginning because I thought anarchists were devilish men who ran around throwing those bowling-ball bombs. But Joe, he was so handsome and enthusiastic and learned.

'Before long money from trade unions, I.W.W. locals, socialist groups and individual donors began to arrive. The mayor got frightened and called out the local militia. Then the governor called out the state police. One afternoon, maybe two weeks into the strike, a parade of strikers was organized. Tens of thousands of us marching down the street together. Chanting, singing, carrying signs.'

Mrs Spanna stopped. She rose from her rocker, walked to the bookcase and removed a large scrapbook. She fanned through a number of pages then brought the book to me and placed it on my lap. It was an old newspaper photograph of a group of women marching down the street holding signs. In the center of the group was a woman whose sign read, GIVE US OUR BREAD AND ROSES. Upon closer examination I recognized Mrs Spanna. 'That's where the strike got its name,' she said, gleaming. 'From that sign, when the photo was printed the following day in the newspaper.' I was struck by the empowered look on Mrs Spanna's face – the picture was old and faded, but the depth of her youthful beauty was obvious. Mrs Spanna took the scrapbook back and returned it to the bookcase, then sat down in her rocker and began right where she had left off.

'Well, we were about half way into the march when the police attacked the parade. There were shots. A young Italian girl was shot and killed. Anna Lo Pizzo. I wasn't near that section of the parade but all accounts I heard from witnesses claimed a policeman did it. No marchers I knew carried weapons. You see from the beginning the strike had an anti-violence platform. That would be its strength. Well, instead of finding the policeman responsible for the shooting, the police arrested and accused Ettor. They also arrested Arturo Giovannitti, a poet, one of the anarchist leaders and a friend of Joe's. The fact is, neither of the accused men were at the scene of the shooting when it happened.

'Well, it seemed like the strike might cave in right then. But they called in Big Bill Haywood and Elizabeth Gurley Flynn, who made fiery speeches at mass rallies. Elizabeth Gurley Flynn was truly inspiring and spoke on everything from worker's rights to women's rights, women's legislation, birth control, which at that time you could get arrested for mentioning in public, prostitution, divorce and free love. Haywood was renowned, and ignited the crowds with attacks on the industries that would steal playtime from children, and I remember his fervor as he raised his fist in the air shouting, "It's time to break the fangs of capitalism." But by then there were over twenty companies of militia and cavalry troops in the city, and martial law was declared. Strikers began to get arrested and sentenced to one-year prison terms. There was a Syrian man, Ramy was his last name. And he was bayoneted to death by army men. But the strikers stayed out. We made signs that read, BAYONETS CANNOT WEAVE CLOTH.

'By the end of February there were mass pickets, ten thousand strikers in an endless chain. But food was running out and children were hungry. That was when *The Call* began to run articles proposing children to be removed from the city and taken in by sympathetic supporters and families. The I.W.W. and socialists began organizing for the exodus of the children from Lawrence. Within a week about one hundred children left on a train for New York City where they were greeted by five thousand Italian socialists singing the "Internationale". There was talk between my aunt and uncle of sending me back to my parents' farm but I wouldn't hear of it. By then I was fully caught up in activity of the strike. And I was falling in love with Joe. The next week one hundred more children were sent to Barre, Vermont.

'It was becoming clear to the authorities that without the worry of the children the strikers could strike indefinitely. So the Lawrence City Officials said that no more children could go. I don't remember exactly how they did that legally, but it was some kind of statute on child neglect. Despite what the officials said, another group of children was organized to go to Philadelphia. When they got to the Railroad Station it was filled with police who closed in on them. They clubbed children and adults without discretion. One week later, a group of women was returning from a meeting, police surrounded them and beat them with clubs. One of the women was pregnant and she lost her baby. But the strikers held out. The more abuses they suffered, the stronger their will to hold out, you see. They were always singing, marching, meeting.

'Finally, the American Woolen Company gave in. They offered raises to all. I don't remember what percentage it was but the strikers insisted that the biggest increases go to the lowest wage earners. The strikers held out for time-and-a-quarter for overtime and no discrimination for those who had participated in the strike, which is what many feared. Well, right about that time, one Sunday afternoon in March, ten thousand strikers gathered on the Common. Big Bill Haywood presided over the gathering and they voted to end the strike. By then, you see, there were some internal struggles developing. Many of the anarchists, most of them atheists, were opposed to the Catholic faction of strikers. The anarchists who were opposed to anarcho-syndicalism still supported the strike, but were opposed to the I.W.W.'s notion of having what the anarchists saw as leaders. They boycotted many of the marches and meetings because most of the parades and meetings were led by leaders, and the anarchists, and Joe certainly fell into this category, were opposed to any sense of hierarchy within the strike force. We got into many heated debates over this. I argued with Joe how could anything be accomplished without some sense of organization, which by its nature implied the necessity of leaders, if nothing else than to represent the strikers in the negotiations? Of course, Joe and I never did see eye to eye on many matters. But the strikers voted to accept the terms and end the strike. That was March 14, 1912.

'It was a huge victory. But it didn't last long. That September, Ettor and Giovannitti went on trial for the murder of Anna Lo Pizzo. Support for them began to mount all over the country. There were huge parades in Boston and New York City. Fifteen thousand Lawrence workers struck for twenty-four hours to show their support. After that about two thousand strikers were fired from their jobs. In support, the I.W.W., who'd grown stronger in Lawrence, threatened to call another mass strike unless the workers were rehired. So they were rehired. When a jury found Ettor and Giovannitti not guilty, ten thousand people gathered on the Lawrence Common to celebrate. I'll never forget that day because somehow I felt that things were really changing, that people could actually make a difference. Instead, in many ways,

"Bread and Roses" was the beginning of the end for the I.W.W. and their "One Big Union". And for the American work force as I knew it then. But it was a great moment that day on the common. The singing and cheering. The speeches. It was my time to be young and alive.'

Mrs Spanna had been talking to a nick-knack mirror on the opposite wall, and she looked at me and smiled. The room was dulling in late-afternoon winter light. I didn't know what to say so I said nothing. Vin interrupted the delicious silence with an 'alas.' I told Mrs Spanna that I hoped we hadn't kept her too late. She told Vin that she thought it was good for Joe to see him that day and that he should come again soon. On the way out the door I wanted to hug her but wasn't sure if it would be appropriate. I thanked her for lunch and when I reached out my hand she took it, shook it, then pulled me towards her for a mutual kiss on the cheek. I developed a crush on her.

Vin said as far as he knew, they were the last of the old-timers around who lived through the Lawrence Strike. I made Vin promise that we'd visit Mrs Spanna again. He said it was too bad Joe had lost his marbles. There were still things he could have learned from him. Within a few weeks we received word that Joe had died of a heart attack. A memorial service was held for him but it was on a weekend and I had to work. I wanted to see Mrs Spanna. Vin reported that Mrs Spanna was holding up well and spoke eloquently about Joe during the memorial service. I couldn't get my mind off her. I'd find myself trying to remember exactly what she looked like in the newspaper photograph. I pressed Vin to take me up to Lawrence to visit her over the next couple of months and for one reason or another it didn't happen. Then one day a phone call came from the Spanna's daughter telling Vin that Mrs Spanna had died the night before in her sleep. She was so healthy it was the last thing we would have thought we'd hear. Vin and I drove up to the poorly-attended service at an ancient funeral home in Lawrence. In the smoking room Vin said when you are Mrs Spanna's age, most of your associates and friends are already dead.

Before we left I walked to the open coffin and took a hard look at Mrs Spanna in an attempt to take in all of her features. Her skin shrunk into her facial bones but she seemed to smile. I thought of my mother and how she looked made-up in her death mask and my father told me they sewed her mouth shut. I leaned over and kissed her cold forehead.

from the Journals of Herbert Minderman:

At the soapbox there were several men in front of me and I waited my turn. Every time one of the men got on the box to speak, policemen surrounded him and pulled him to the ground and they hit him with clubs and tossed him into the police wagon. When it was my turn the police asked me how old I was and I told them nineteen. I began my speech about my right to free speech and they hauled me down and hit me with their clubs. The wagon was so full we had one difficult time breathing, being so packed in as we were. At the station they jammed us into one holding cell and we rotated around two benches. The men not sitting stood squeezed against each other. There was no food, water, or means to relieve ourselves. In the morning they removed us to the courtroom, two and three at a time. I practiced the tactic of taking as much time as possible during my hearing, and it took an afternoon before I received my sentence of sixty days. Twice as long as my first. In the cell there were two sets of bunks and men stood bunched together. We rotated the bunks one hour in, three hours standing. A tall, muscular fellow with a face that looked like it had been through a hurricane stretched his hand out to me and introduced himself as Frank Little. The Frank Little. I would have been beaten up a hundred times over to share a cell with Hobo Frank Little. We made him talk about the struggles with the Western Federation of Miners, the Missoula fight for the Lumberjacks, and the Spokane free speech fight. He lifted his shirt and his pants legs and showed us which bone had been broken in which fight. But here let me say, that Frank Little is the humblest of men, and it was only upon much encouragement from the men in the cell did he share his stories with us. They brought us old bread and one watered down cup of soup per man for supper. That night I slept next to Frank Little. His body was like iron. Who would believe it. Next to me on the floor was Hobo Frank Little. In the morning they took him away and a deafening cheer rang out from the prisoners. 'Frank. Frank. Frank. Frank.'

Diary of Christina Donato:

'We are betrayed. Ricardo keeps a pair of diamond earrings from Christmas Eve and brings them to a fence in South Boston, unaware that the fence is working for the police. The Christmas Eve home is owned by the former state Attorney General, and the police have been working the streets, raiding fences and offering them protection if they report seeing any of the loot. Fortunately, Ricardo doesn't know where the press is located. But he could identify Fillipo, Antonio and myself as accomplices in the heist. If the police find material related to the movement in Ricardo's room, he will be implicated in the movement. Antonio says Ricardo will not talk. I'm not so sure. Neither is Fillipo. We move the loot and all literature from my room. Carlo has a friend in Lawrence who allows us the use of his attic. Fillipo borrows an automobile and we load it with all the issues of The Watchdog *and other literature, the last of the jewelry, and a fur coat. Carlo's friend is married to a lovely Polish woman who works in a wool mill. They are veterans of the Bread and Roses Strike who invite us to lunch, and over a delicious soup we plan our next move. We do not know what Ricardo has told the police. Without any loot, they won't be able to hold us. On his friend's invitation, Carlo remains in Lawrence. He does not want to be away from me right now, but it is safer. The rest of us return to Somerville and sit quietly. The mornings are the toughest time for me right now as I wake up sick to my stomach. It is good that Carlo is in Lawrence because the news of my pregnancy has made him crazy. He insists that we should marry. Then in the next breath claims that marriage and parenting are not for the revolutionary. It's all or nothing for him. He believes a true revolutionary must not be swayed from his cause for the sake of love. Revolutionaries should not become too attached to anything or anyone. But I am a human being first. I will have the child and I will raise the child. He hit me with his*

open hand. I hit him over the head with a skillet. His head bled. He writes from Lawrence that I must forgive him for hurting me. He is tired of running and we should sail for Italy as soon as we can.'

The Memoirs of Errico Malatesta, Early Years

The Naples police post a guard to arrest anyone who comes to claim the mail of D. Pasqualio. I have been informed that every morning at ten-fifteen, the guard leaves his position for ten minutes. The large round clock above the post-office door reads 10:15. One minute later, the guard leaves the post office and walks down the block to a café. Because the police fear that some postal workers might be sympathetic to the movement, they have not informed the postal clerks of their trap. I enter the post office undetected, and there is a line.

A woman argues with a clerk who insists that she rewrap her package. The woman shouts at him, she says that yesterday another clerk told her to wrap the package this way. The clerk calls for the senior clerk.

The guard has a description of me; so, I must be out on time. The senior officer insists that the woman rewrap the package. She curses the men, and their families, may they die the worst of deaths and kiss her ass.

The line moves quickly. At the window I ask for letters addressed to D. Pasqualio. The clerk returns with several. I leave in time to see the guard walking towards the post office and I turn and rush off in the opposite direction.

My time in Naples is limited. I hide out in the home of friends; but I cannot place them at risk any further. The government has decreed the dissolution of hundreds of republican and internationalist societies throughout the country; their members are being persecuted, jailed, and in some instances killed.

Unfortunately, the masses continue to remain indifferent. The three major bulletins which expound the new revolutionary ideas have not been widely distributed. In any event, too many peasants are illiterate and cannot read our bulletins.

We were too optimistic. In the south, we placed our hopes in men who had never been tested; such men we didn't know well enough. We made the mistake of taking Bakunin's doctrines on faith. But, this is our tradition; have not all of the insurrections of this century, those of Mazzini and Garibaldi, ended in such a way? We can profit from all agitation, even the failures. One by one they add up, and will lead, to a widespread popular movement.

Although we are a handful, the public will talk about us as they do today, and our attempts are at least effective propaganda. It is our aim that everybody should become socially conscious and effective. But in order to achieve this it is necessary to destroy with violence, since one cannot do otherwise, the violence which denies these means to the masses.

Of course, a successful insurrection is the most potent factor in the emancipation of the people. But the people are unaware of the real reasons for their misery. They have always wanted very little, and have achieved very little. What will they want from the next insurrection? That will depend on our propaganda and what efforts we are able to put into it now. Everything depends on what the people are capable of wanting.

I stare at the textured ceiling over my bed. With every noise, flit of a bird, voice or footsteps in the street, I expect the authorities to knock. Tomorrow I will leave Naples, make my way north, and eventually cross over the border into Switzerland. I will be able to continue my work there.

The bell from a nearby church rings every quarter of an hour. Four times per hour, twenty-four hours per day, the church bell rings. Now, that is what I mean by effective propaganda!

■ ■ ■

When the novelty of having me around wore off, Vin returned to his regular routines. In the morning we drank espresso laced with anisette while Vin made or waited for his daily calls from various friends and contacts in California, Mexico, New York City, Italy, France or Pakistan. Conversations were research-related; either he was looking for some information, or giving it. Vin was always writing an article or review for an obscure journal. Often I helped with editing as he frequently wrote twenty-five thousand words for five-thousand-word articles. After talking on the phone, he packed his briefcase and left, returning after midnight, when he would go into his study and work until three or four in the morning. The next morning he informed me of the previous day's events: he was involved in an argument with the director of archives at the Boston Public Library; he met Julio for drinks and dined with Gianni and their friends Alice and Tony who were in town from San Diego; there was a meeting at the Dante Society and he told off the new director; later he went to hear Ray Santisi perform a solo piano gig at a club and after the gig he and Ray went to some eatery where lots of the musicians gather for a late snack and drinks.

During that period of time, outside of the dishwashing job on weekends, I barely left Vin's apartment. After Vin went out in the morning I browsed through books and journals, played music and drank. I worked my way through the stacks in Vin's study room and explored his microfilm archive. There was so much material I don't know how Vin kept track but he said it was all in his head. I found complete runs of anarchist newspapers and literature dating back to the mid-nineteenth century. There were writings in English, Italian, French, Polish, Greek. Yards of files and films on the Sacco and Vanzetti case including trial transcripts, defense investigations, correspondences, newspaper and magazine articles from all over the world. The files contained dozens of familiar names and names I didn't know, like Carlo Valdinoci and Christina Donato. Vin had mentioned Valdinoci on our Vermont trip and through my Valdinoci investigations I discovered Christina Donato, a.k.a. Rossa Nero, cross-filed with *The Watchdog*, a Somerville anarchist press publishing literature and a newsletter in English from 1916–1919. Later I made the connection between the name Donato and the maiden name I'd seen on Vin's mother's death certificate when I packed up her things and brought them to the basement. I went down to the basement to double-check I had remembered it correctly – Emma Donato.

I made no mention of any of this to Vin, though suspicion led me to re-examine the contents of the box. Among the crucifix and other personal belongings there was an old worn photograph of two young couples standing side by side. It might have been any two couples during the early part of the century in Sunday clothing and at an outdoor event, smiling like they still knew a speckle of innocence, the men gripping mugs of ale. There wasn't much to distinguish any of them but several things about the couple on the left held my eye: the man's crooked smile and thick hair, his bushy eyebrows, stocky frame and broad shoulders; the woman's slightly crossed eyes, thin-lipped smile and birth mark on her forehead.

Friday afternoon Vin met with several men he referred to as 'the group', which was made up of five or six regulars, and others who came and went. They gathered at an Italian restaurant in what was once Somerville's meat-packing district, a workingman's place, serving pizza, sandwiches and pasta with red sauce. The men ate, drank, smoked, and talked idle gossip to present-day events, sitting around a double-sized wooden booth until early evening when they continued with drinks and more food at another location. Many dicey arguments led to shouting matches and the owner of the restaurant, a chubby, balding but tolerant old man, frequently came out of the kitchen to quiet things down. I said little. The arguments followed the same circular patterns and I learned the arguing tactics of each of the men and I could predict what one of them would say and when they would say it.

There was Julio, a Mexican sculptor, about forty years old, a good-looking, dark-skinned, black-haired man who taught at Mass. College of Art. Alec, the others referred to as a Stalinist but he called himself a Trotskyite, a tiny pale man of about sixty years with wire-rimmed glasses and dirty clothes, whose bald scalp flaked in droves. Raffaelo was the poet who had attended the Dante meetings Carol hosted at our apartment. He taught poetry in inner-city high schools and claimed to be a nephew of Carlo Tresca. He kept up a correspondence with Carol and he never failed to remind me. Have you heard from Carol? Oh, I got a letter from her the other day. Clifford was an English teacher at Roxbury Community College, a heavy black man in his middle fifties who never smiled. He was a writer and photographer. His photographs of workers who were victims of a fatal lung disease caused by exposure to asbestos were published and won him some acclaim. Finally there was Nunzio Zarella, the retired shoemaker, a man with a great laugh and tremendous appetite who took his pleasure scoffing at anything any of the others said.

These were the founders of the *Black Rose* group, who ran a lecture series and from 1975 to 1985 and published a quarterly magazine by the same name. I wondered how they ever got one issue off the ground. Disagreements over art finally splintered the group and caused the magazine's demise; half of the men were opposed to abstract art because they considered it bourgeois – the other half wanted to use abstract art. I couldn't imagine the concept of abstract art being any kind of issue by the 1970s, but each man drew his own lines.

A Month of Trials and Sentences: Film Maker Sentenced to 10 Years; 101 Wobblies, Max Eastman and Floyd Dell

The *U.S. v. Spirit of '76* case has ended with the maker of the film *The Spirit of '76* found guilty. William Taggart, who made the movie which depicts British atrocities against the colonists during the American Revolution has received a ten-year prison sentence. Judge George. F. Bell said the film questioned 'the good faith of our ally, Great Britain'.

The mass trial has begun for 101 of the 165 I.W.W. leaders arrested last September in raids throughout the country. The leaders are charged with conspiring to hinder the draft, encouraging desertion and intimidating others in connection with labor disputes. One of the first to take the stand and testify was Big Bill Haywood. His testimony lasted for three days. The trial of lumberjacks, harvesters, miners, editors, longshoreman and factory workers is expected to last through the summer. Some say it may be the longest criminal trial in the history of the United States.

In the words of one of the accused: 'If every person who represented law and order in the nation beat you up, railroaded you to jail, and the good Christian people cheered and told them to go to it, how the hell do you expect a man to be patriotic? This war is a business man's war and we don't see why we should go out and get shot in order to save the lovely state of affairs that we now enjoy.'

In New York City the trial of Max Eastman, Floyd Dell and other editors of *The Masses* has begun. The men are being tried for conspiracy to obstruct military recruiting. The United States Post Office has already banned *The Masses* from the mails, but the paper continues to publish and distribute. Journalist John Reed, recently returned from

Russia where he reported on the Bolshevik Revolution, is covering the mass I.W.W. Trial for *The Masses*.

All over the country, teachers and institutional administrators are being put out of their jobs for their opposition to the war. The number of people being prosecuted under the Espionage Act continues to multiply, as does the death toll of the young men in Europe who are dying. Each edition of *The Watchdog* could be the last. Attorney General Palmer has stated himself that 'never in its history has the country been so thoroughly policed.' This is a police state. We must remain united in our cause and Resist!

– Rossa Nero

May 1, 1918

Dearest Tina,

Tomorrow I leave for Vermont. The harsh weather conditions have prevented an earlier departure. Now that the spring has arrived, I will find El Vecc. My friend will first take me to visit my mother, and then leave me at the Vermont border. These people have been gracious hosts; but I can impose on them no longer. I must see you before I leave. Please, reconsider, and return to Italy with me and the child. You say that this is your country and there is work to be done here. The revolution should recognize no boundaries. The walls of nationalism must crumble to dust in order to necessitate a new vision. We would be freer to do our work in Italy. As it is, I am unable to walk down the street for fear that I am being followed. I hope that you will think of the child's future. If you are discovered, you will end up in jail. And what of the child then? You have the name and address where you can reach me at El Vecc's. Keep me informed of your health and the progress. My hands are tied. There is nothing more that I can do for the movement here. El Vecc has written to me, if his connections remain in place, there is a possibility that in the autumn I might cross the border into Canada and find a ship that will take me to South America or Italy. These past months I have had much time to organize some of my ideas. If I have the opportunity to write during the summer, I will forward the work. You and the child remain foremost in my thoughts. If only I had the stone will of our Russian friends who for the cause put human sentiments of pleasure, love, passion and attachment aside.

  All my love,
  Carlo

■ ■ ■

'I don't have these narrow, rigid views that I try to force on reality, like some people. But there are things about our society that are pretty obvious, and people walk around with blinders on – or worse, are simply indifferent. If you're thinking about the future, you can't consume the present. Alas, this is the age of consumerism, so no one can think about the future. Everywhere you hear of progress, progress. Progress for what? For who? More often than not what's brought into this world in the name of progress ends up having the opposite effect. Gunpowder. Or more recently, radar. Radar was invented to detect German submarines in World War I. Now it's being used by fisherman all over the world and they're depleting all the fish in the ocean, which might spell the end of mankind as we know it. The oceans are so noisy the whales can't hear their love calls. What kind of world is this? Humans have already taken the planet too far. Each generation should treat it like a garden, leaving it a little better than they found it. But people have no collective memory. It's all madness. There's no sense of where we're coming from or where we are headed. No idea of the *individual*, *action*, the *social* within society. Christ, with all this Yuppie gluttony for things – there's no evidence to me of an understanding of the real *pleasures* of life. I mean this nouvelle cuisine thing – I can't stand it – it's politicizing food – 'Nice presentation' – I can't stand that term. No one understands good food any longer. The media makes celebrities of all these chefs – if they were in France or Italy they'd still be cutting up vegetables. There's just no sense to it. No feel for good food, good friends, good music. Everything is driven by money. There's no such thing as workers taking pleasure in what they do. Now it's just a job. All these

Yuppies talking about early retirement. For what? What will they do? Sex has been taken away and become this abstract, politicized thing. And now with AIDS, who knows what will happen. As we come closer to the end of the millennium, it's only getting worse. People are going to become more desperate because there's no emotion left. The majority of people in this country still believe in religious miracles – the Devil and resurrection and God intervening in personal and global matters. These same people make out Muslims in the Middle East to be religious fanatics! And the God and Country routine the Republicans are playing out since their convention – if you look back, only fifty years, you'll see that Hitler's speeches during the nineteen-thirties weren't much different from much of the rhetoric spewed out at the Republican convention. You know what Huey Long said, when Fascism comes to America, it'll be wrapped in an American flag. And as people become more alienated and isolated they'll be more irrational, wanting more than what they're getting on television. Constructive ways of living will be cut off. All this virtual reality stuff you hear as if reality is *over there*. People will be having sex with their goddamned computers. You'll see a return to religion and cults. Mark my words. And they'll make sense as people will believe they have fewer and fewer choices. Remember that the Roman Empire fell from within, not from without. But alas, my dear Gregorio, it comes back as it always does, to history. There's just no sense of it. Not that we should live in the past, but if we can save the past, we might be able to cast a different light on it and save the future. But people are numb. This Savings and Loan thing. The media makes it look like there are a few people responsible. They'll be given a slap on their wrists and be taking limos to expensive restaurants in no time. This scam goes all the way to the top, but the media won't investigate it that far, and if they did, they'd never report it. I mean this God-damned Iran-Contra. Christ, even those who love Reagan believe that he knew – but they shrug their shoulders and think that's just the way things are. What this president has done is far worse than what Nixon did. But that shows how much the country's temperament has shifted over the past twenty years. They'll let this North guy take the rap and Reagon will come out of it clean. And Bush claiming that he didn't know, how could he not have known? And if he didn't, how could he have been so out of touch that he didn't know? Christ, this country is still backing South Africa. Who cares? Or knows about it? The government can only rule when they control public opinion, which they've managed to do since World War I when the Creel Commission turned an anti-war population into a country of people who wanted to destroy anything German. And after the war the government used the same media control to instigate the Red Scare. People don't understand these things. The Red Scare effectively destroyed unions, free press, and the freedom of political thought, sixty years ago. These programs pushed through by the Reagan administration – are they really as popular as they're reported to be? Do Americans really want cutbacks on their children's education, or health care, or welfare? The polls actually show that the majority of Americans prefer spending money on social services over spending on the military. But the media makes it look as if these people are the minority. Christ, Reagan won by a three to two margin in the eighty-four election and the media reported it as a landslide. But when you control the media, and you control education with scholarship which is nothing but conformist, you can effectively falsify history, so there's this warped view of the actual facts. Alas, and the minority of those in the country, the ones who've decided to find some kind of alternative, are all caught up in this New Age oneness and wave of mysticism which is just another sign of social decay. A form of social deception. So self-absorbed and self-absorbing. It's not a matter of waiting for any kind of social upheaval – they don't even want it. They denounce technology and the system but have good cars, expensive stereos and professional jobs. I saw an ad last week for a ten-thousand-dollar stereo. Who spends ten thousand dollars for a stereo? What does it do? Style over substance. Middle-class rebels who turn vegetarian and shop at expensive natural food stores and boutiques. Well, there's no sense of aesthetics. And the young generation. Everything seems lost on them. It's all just instant gratification, these kids with the purple hair. It used to be taste was something that you cultivated through experience, whether it be with food, or with clothing. Now there's no such thing as taste. The buds are gone. Generation by generation things are spiraling ever-downward. Well, in the end, the human race might just be unremarkable. Part of a universal food chain. Everything's diminishing step by step, you can see it if you look. The rhythms are disappearing. Used to be there was a sense of seasons. The peasants knew it. And the end of the peasantry and the advent of the machine mark the last great landmark losses for human civilization, at least as I see it. The peasants had a feel for the land. They knew that if you didn't properly care for the land this year, you didn't eat the next. Even when people began to move from the farms to industry, there was a sense that you had a job to do and a life to live, there was a rhythm and pleasure to it. When you shopped at the market you bought produce that was seasonal and grown regionally. Now, Christ, you go to the market and you get plums from Chile in the middle of the winter, some obscure fruit from an Indian island ends up on dessert plate in a fancy Boston restaurant. But it has no taste. In the old days, for a few weeks a year, you got to eat real Georgia peaches and knew that only in those precious weeks you could take pleasure in those peaches. But now, it's all just a mishmash. There's so much but really so little. If anything, Gregorio, leisure time should be more important than work time. But instead of opposing uniformity people embrace it – our culture is one of a work ethic. There's no such thing as human diversity and a richness of being. It'll take generations to undo what Reagan did in the past eight years, and he did one fine job on your generation. Everyone wants to be a stock broker. Everybody acts as if capitalism has *won* now that the communist states are falling. What *winning* will mean for countries like Russia and East Germany and China will be a form of institutionalized looting. Alas, language is breaking down. In the old days you could have clear arguments. People were able to have intelligent discussions. You could debate, say, ballet vs. modern dance with two clear, different viewpoints. But it would be an *exchange* – and you could see that even though one is markedly different from the other, somehow they corresponded. But there's no longer any such thing as a clear sense of judgement or a sense of a natural order emerging – everything is just silting up like a big sewer pipe spilling sludge from everywhere.'

The Memoirs of Errico Malatesta, Early Years

At the conductor's last call I breathe easier. The boy sitting next to me says that he travels to Rome to visit relatives. Across from us an attractive well-dressed couple is seated, they are returning to Florence from holiday on the southern coast and speak Florentine, assuming that the boy and I travel together and speak a southern dialect, and I don't understand them.

I wear an ill-fitting suit borrowed from a friend in Naples. The boy is dressed in a country outfit he might wear to church on Sunday; he is groomed, but his fingernails hold traces of dirt. The couple is angry, because of a confusion in the train seating, they are forced to travel the crowded train in the lower-class coach.

Naples and the bay slowly disappear from sight as the train rolls into the rocky landscape towards Rome; Vesuvius looms large but, as the train speeds faster, it eventually recedes into the background.

The woman complains. Her husband holds her hand. The boy removes a knife, some bread, and piece of dried sausage from a rough leather bag and begins to eat, tearing the bread and cutting the sausage with his knife.

At each stop I strain nervously to look out on to the platform. Villages roll into crop fields which roll into villages. Hundreds upon hundreds of peasants are bent over the land.

I shift my weight from one buttock to the other on the hard wooden bench. The farther north we travel, the greener and more lush the landscape; and, as we approach Rome, the clusters of villages and farms are closer together with more workers visible in the fields. The boy removes a wooden soldier from his bag and pretends to shoot at people in the fields. I question the boy, why does he shoot at those people? He says it is only make believe; and, besides, he does not know them.

The train slows as we approach Rome. My lungs are wheezing. Ancient viaducts reach out in every direction and larger buildings appear, thousands of years of building, layer upon layer. In Rome it will be one hour until my next train departs. Tomorrow I will cross the border into Switzerland.

I sit for an hour with my back against a pillar on a platform bench. The next train is half full, and I fall into a light sleep at the outer limits of Rome. The train builds up speed; I sway to the motion. When I next open my eyes I look upon a flat valley, the Arno River, and distant low-lying Tuscan hills. Everywhere grape clusters burst on vines and the smell is strong enough to chew. On the hilltops the old estates sit in all their majesty.

At the Florence station, families greet loved ones. A handsome young man finds his way into the arms of a buxom, teary-eyed woman. I remove the pipe from my jacket and fill it.

Someone is next to me. He is a man of about fifty years, hunched over as if he's been far too long at a task he is not fit for. He tells me to follow him, and through the crowded station we walk out to a small café on an alley one block away.

We sit at an outside table. I eat bread, cheese and wine. The stranger speaks about the failure of the recent insurrection in the north. Everything that could have gone wrong, did go wrong. Where there were men, there were no arms. Too many groups failed to come through, or follow up on initial successes. The various Florentine leaders of the Italian Federation were in jail, or had fled the area.

In Rimini, I am to leave the station and walk to a small café on Via Antinori. I will recognize the place by a small brass bell that hangs over the door. I will sit down at the table in the corner by the window, order a glass of wine, and tell the keeper to make certain the wine is from his private barrel. Until then, I am to trust no one.

I bid the man a farewell with hopes that our next meeting will be under more favorable circumstances. In the distance, I see the top half of Giotto's Tower. In my youth, I attempted to climb it; but I was overcome with anxiety before I reached the top and I collapsed on the steps in a fit of coughing.

The Notebooks

'... They tell us that we live in a great free republic; that our institutions are democratic; that we are a free and self-governing people. That is too much, even for a joke ... Wars throughout history have been waged for conquest and plunder ... And that is war in a nutshell. The master class has always declared wars, the subject class has always fought the battles ... Yes, in good time we are going to sweep into power in this nation and throughout the world. We are going to destroy all enslaving and degrading capitalist institutions and re-create them as free and humanizing institutions. The world is daily changing before our eyes. The sun of capitalism is setting; the sun of Socialism is rising ... In due time the hour will strike and this great cause triumphant will proclaim the emancipation of the working class and the brotherhood of all mankind ...'

Diary of Christina Donato:

'When the police raid my room they find nothing to implicate me in connection with the robbery. They take me to the station for questioning. In return for a lighter sentence for dealing in stolen merchandise, Ricardo has named his accomplices. But Fillipo, Antonio and I deny any connection with the robbery, and acknowledge knowing Ricardo as an acquaintance only. Antonio's girlfriend will testify that he was with her the entire evening. Fillipo and I will claim that we were together on Christmas Eve, along with two comrades who have agreed to swear to it. Ricardo has not disclosed anything about the movement or our involvement in it. He knows that if he is implicated in the movement, he will be prosecuted under the Espionage Act no matter what he tells the police. At the station I am interviewed by a detective and a matron. The matron pretends to be sympathetic, the detective is tough. He wants to know how long I have known Ricardo. What was I doing Christmas Eve? When was the last time I was in Milton? When was the last time I saw Ricardo? Did I see Ricardo on Christmas Eve? Wasn't it true that I took part in the robbery and that my room was used to store the loot? He wants to know who the father of my child is. I tell him that it is a local boy, a grocer's son who volunteered and is now fighting on the front in France. We had one last night before he left for Europe and he doesn't know of my condition. What is the boy's name? I give them the name of the grocer on Somerville Avenue, his son is serving in France. The detective asks how I support myself. I write and translate for Italian immigrants, many of whom are illiterate. Several hours pass this way until the detective says I am free to go but I must make myself available for further questioning. The spring air is refreshing. All the shops are closed in Union Square, the clerk is asleep at his desk in the Union Square Hotel. I walk down Somerville Avenue and I turn the detective's questions over and *examine all of my answers. My pregnancy and the story of the baby's father fighting at the front are my salvation. At home I sit down to a cup of tea. There is a knock on the door. Fillipo has been detained for several hours of grueling questions; but he believes that he has been cleared. They have no evidence but Ricardo's word. We fear that we will be under surveillance, so we must suspend the publication of* The Watchdog. *We cannot run the risk of having the location of the press detected. Because of our haul on Christmas Eve, there is still enough money for several more issues and to cover our living expenses until the fall. We are both tired. Fillipo and I slip into bed. He holds me tight around the waist. The baby is kicking and turning. Fillipo chuckles. This baby has a lot of life, am I sure that it is not his. I say nothing. An airplane flies overhead low and loud. Fillipo begins to snore after it passes. Carlo is somewhere in Vermont. In France, the grocer's son, full of holes face down in mud.'*

Eugene Debs Arrested

Eugene Debs was arrested in Canton, Ohio, after delivering a speech in which he spoke out against the war. Debs was in Canton in support of three Socialists who are currently in jail for opposing the draft. After visiting the three men in jail, Debs made his speech across the street from the jail house. According to the authorities, there were draft-age youths in attendance, and Debs words would 'obstruct the recruiting or enlistment service'.

If convicted, Debs, who received nearly one million votes in his presidential campaign in 1912, will face up to twenty years in prison. In a statement Debs said, 'I am opposed to every war but one; I am for that war with heart and soul, and that is the world-wide war of the social revolution.'

President Wilson and Attorney General Palmer continue to wage their war at home. More I.W.W. union halls, socialist, anarchist and communist presses and headquarters have been raided, more men and women arrested and jailed. As of this month, *The Watchdog* will no longer publish monthly because of a lack of finances and the tightening government noose. We will continue our efforts when finances and freedom permit. We must continue the struggle on all fronts, and remember our comrades who have suffered and continue to suffer.

– Rossa Nero

The Notebooks

'... When Louis Brusa came to Barre as a teenaged Italian immigrant at the turn of the century he joyfully looked forward to making granite tell a story through the skill of his hands. For years as a working partner at Brusa Brothers, the family stoneshed on Blackwell Street, he watched the stone chips fly away under his compressed-air tools without fully grasping that the clouds of resulting stone dust would one day be his undoing ... The hill stood quiet as they gouged out its stone, yet it was not without revenge. In the end, stone took its toll on all stonecutters ... By 1895, the monument industry had become the mainstay of Barre's economy and a far-sighted committee began to plan Hope Cemetery that year ... It was rumored that it was one of the Communist faction that were responsible for the raid on *Cronaca Sovversiva*. In return for key information, Flavio Bernadina was not prosecuted under the Espionage Act ... He was no hypocrite. He believed in the noble objective of his work. The fact that he and Galleani were in opposition had no bearing on his actions. He knew what was coming was inevitable, and it could be said he saved Galleani by not naming the location of his hideout ... Before the coming of the motor vehicle, watering troughs were as essential as the gas stations of today. In the late 19th century, the crossroads intersection at the center of downtown Barre featured a large watering trough. Unfortunately, it was not until the automobile made its debut in 1911 that Barre received an elegant granite-and-bronze watering trough, a bequest of the founder the National Humane Alliance . . . Upon completion of the Skyline railroad to the quarries, the surrounding area became crowded with granite sheds . . . Less than a year later, Bernadina was arrested, and eventually deported with a number of other socialists and Communists . . . Built to accommodate an innovative hoisting system, this 16-sided shed was the prototype of what was to come . . . It was agreed that the burial ground should be directly adjacent with the church . . . It took a long time for marble and slate to give way to granite . . .'

September 1918, Barre, Vermont

There is a house without straight edges. Floors, doors, windows, frames, walls, support beams, the chimney: not one straight edge. Nothing but individually constructed units designed to unique specifications melding with adjacent counter-parts. Chairs, table, shelves, sink and stove – no corners but curves, round surfaces rolling into a wavy circumflexion. Carlo Valdinoci runs his hand along the surfaces and contours.

Smell of coffee. Sound of dishes and pots. He opens his eyes. The cottage consists of a kitchen area and two rooms for sleeping. The granite worker who owns the woods cottage has allowed Luigi Galleani and his family to live here in hiding. Carlo shares sleeping quarters with Galleani's two sons who are sitting at the table with Galleani. Luigi's wife Bonita pours a cup of coffee for Carlo and places a warm biscuit on a plate.

At the table Galleani explains that the headquarters of *Cronaca Sovversiva* was raided the night before and police took Giusseppe Coletti and Lorenzo Paini in for questioning. Because of the nature of the paper's stand against the war, the men were threatened with arrest under the Espionage Act. For some unknown reason, the authorities let them go. All of the paper's correspondences have been confiscated and the printing press dismantled. There is no choice, Galleani says we must leave at nightfall.

During the summer, Carlo and Galleani worked to see *Cronaca Sovversiva* into publication. Galleani wrote articles, Carlo helped with the typesetting. Afternoons they took long walks into the hills, discussing the movement. From the first time he met El Vecc, Carlo was drawn to Galleani's vehement anti-syndicalist views and his uncompromising belief that anarchism alone promotes and realizes the emancipation of mankind. El Vecc rejected all forms of authority, including centralized organizations proposed by the socialists, communists and syndicalists. The anarchist movement and the labor movement followed two parallel lines which geometrically could never meet.

Moreover, and more urgent, they believe in the theory of propaganda by deed. Carlo presses Luigi with questions. When is the effective time to strike? Who should be a target? They walk a familiar path through a stand of evergreens into a valley and a fast-running cold water stream. Galleani limps slightly, an injury he carried since he was shot in the Paterson, New Jersey weavers' strike in 1902. Galleani says he will take his family to New York City, from there, Canada. He has secured for Carlo transportation to Boston where he can hide for a time then sneak to New York City. It would not be good for the movement for the both of them to be caught at the same time. They have important work to do. Carlo kneels down stream-side and takes a long cold drink. It leaves a sharp pain in his head.

∎∎∎

Vin was generous with his time and money. Though I don't know where the latter came from, he always had some cash in his wallet and insisted on buying the drinks or coffee. Any time of the day or night his phone could ring with a call from a friend, frequently with a computer problem, and if Vin couldn't walk them through the problem over the phone he'd be right over.

He did months of work helping the local Italian community make a desktop book of photos, stories and memoirs from residents. There was a Japanese woman, a musician who spoke little English and was having trouble with her green-card status. I assumed they were intimately involved though Vin denied it. Standing in line with her at bureaucratic offices became his regular practice for a time. She was a widow evicted from her apartment and Vin said that she had nobody here to help. And there was an Italian immigrant who never learned to speak English and wrote a book about his childhood memories from Cassino during World War II; he saved a little money and was going to see the book into publication on a vanity press but needed an English translator. Vin worked for six months translating the book and never took a penny.

In 1989 a friend of a friend of Vin's approached him. She was seeking information about her brother who died in 1975. The brother was older and left home when she was five years old. Being Italian immigrants of the old school, her parents disowned the brother because of his lifestyle, which they viewed as unsavory. Vin was no private eye, he told her, but he'd see what he could do. The brother used aliases during his lifetime. Vin took all the information he could from the sister, and over the next several weeks he and I began tracking down leads which led us to assorted state and federal institutions. At Boston City Hall, we located the man's death certificate. The name on the certificate was an alias, with the man's parents and place of birth listed as unknown and the cause of death written as *Ingestion of large amounts of Doriden.*

I learned to keep my mouth shut when I accompanied Vin to enquire about the brother's records. My approach was to walk up to a clerk and disclose every last bit of information, only to find a clerk unaccommodating. After our first encounter, Vin told me that if I was to come along on these excursions, I must keep my mouth shut since my all-informative style wasn't going to get us anywhere. Years of dealing with the authorities over federal and state records taught Vin to reveal as little as possible when conferring with them. He offered a crumb of information at a time. Eventually he could wear down any clerk and have enough in his pocket to overcome any last objection or negations. At a Federal Records Office we viewed records of the man's court trials and later spoke with people who'd known him.

In the end it was enough to help the woman piece together her brother's adult life. He was a poet and some people we interviewed had signed copies of his little books, letters, notebooks and journals which the sister was welcome to view. He was a homosexual addicted to street drugs, served time in prison and institutions for mental health problems. He was also admired by poets and friends and those in the street community of petty thieves, prostitutes and runaways. We acquired copies of the brother's books and several photographs for which his sister was grateful.

One day during our investigation Vin and I were walking down Tremont Street discussing the numerous lives that go unnoticed but are kept alive in little books, letters or photographs held sacred by friends and family. Suddenly, shoes glistening, slick trenchcoat open over designer suit, Newbury Street haircut, expensive briefcase in hand, a man about my age power-walked by us with his arm extended as he checked the time on his wristwatch. It was a glorious afternoon, warm for late March and the sun fashioned mirrors on the Hancock Tower. I didn't think Vin saw the man until without missing a beat he said, 'Now *there's* a man making his way purposefully through life.'

On the outskirts of the North End we decided to get a pizza at the old Regina. We walked down Hanover Street then cut down a small side street to Salem. Vin wanted to get a loaf of bread. New restaurants were springing up everywhere. Grocers, butchers, smoke shops and druggists replaced by upscale eateries with high-priced menus hanging in the windows. At the spot where Di Pietro's Bread used to stand, we were face-to-face with another restaurant.

'I can't believe it,' Vin said, shielding his eyes from the sun to look inside the window at the fine linen tablecloths, shiny silverware and sparkling round wine goblets on the tables. Vin scratched his head and a blizzard of dandruff blew up around him. He looked up Salem Street, then down Salem Street. Restaurants as far as we could see. 'It's gone completely downhill since the mob left.'

from The Journals of Herbert Minderman:

The city officials and leaders of the Local 66 are negotiating. City authorities refuse to compromise under pressure. In order to save face in public, they have agreed to talk with our leaders in secret. Several days ago a local committee of citizens visited the jail to speak with some of our leaders here. They were trying to determine what are our specific truce terms. Since the visit things have changed. Now we eat three times a day. In the morning biscuits and coffee. At lunch soup with brown bread and more cofee. Dinner is stew with real meat with bread and coffee. The men were given back blankets and mattresses. The cells remain overcrowded but we are warm and the hunger cramps are gone. This afternoon we sang songs and cheered the triumph of free speech. Not once did the sheriff or any of his guards attempt to shut us up. Many of the fruit packers are looking ahead to organize themselves when this struggle is finished. If we win this battle, we can wage another in the countryside where it is needed most.

Debs Sentenced to 10, Haywood Gets 20; 164 Found Guilty!

Eugene Debs' case before the United States Supreme Court ended in July with a guilty verdict. Accused of violating the Espionage Act in a public speech, Debs refused to take the stand in his own defense. He also refused to call any witnesses in his defense and to deny what he'd said in his speech. He's been sentenced to 10 years in the federal penitentiary. Debs will appeal the verdict.

In a related case, the longest criminal case ever held in the United States, Big Bill Haywood and 164 other I.W.W. leaders were found guilty under the Espionage Act. Haywood and 14 others were given the maximum of 20 years in prison. 33 were given 10 years, and the rest shorter sentences. The 165 were fined a total of $2,500,000! Haywood has jumped bail.

In one year President Wilson and his leading henchman Attorney General Palmer have successfully dismantled the I.W.W. organization in the United States. Under the Espionage Act, hundreds of innocent people have been subject to unfair beatings, unfair trials, long jail sentences and worse.

The I.W.W., like many other organizations for poor and working people in this country, operates under the laws of this country. As the government has shattered the last vestiges of legal organizations here, they have pushed the poor and working class into a corner. As the revolution in Russia takes hold, we in the United States should look to it as a model. The masses shall not be stifled! If we cannot make change within the legal system, we shall make change outside of it!

– Rossa Nero

The Notebooks

'. . . I have been accused of obstructing the war. I admit it. Gentlemen, I abhor war. I would oppose war if I stood alone . . . I have sympathy with the suffering, struggling people everywhere. It does not make any difference under what flag they were born, or where they live . . . Your honor, years ago I recognized my kinship with all living beings, and I made up my mind that I was not one bit better than the meanest on earth. I said then, and I say now, that while there is a lower class, I am in it; while there is a criminal element, I am of it; while there is a soul in prison, I am not free . . . I denounce those who would strike the sword from the hand of this nation while she is engaged in defending herself against a foreign and brutal power . . .'

The Memoirs of Errico Malatesta, Early Years

At the Rimini Police Headquarters I am questioned in a small windowless room. The captain sits across from me, between us is a table on which the contents of my leather bag sit: 1,200 lire, a revolver, pipe, tobacco, a code and two letters.

The captain asks me my name and I tell him Domenic Pasqualio. He says he already knows my real name. So, I say, why do you ask me then if you think you already know?

He is curious why I carry no identification. I have no need. What is my purpose in Rimini? I am on my way to Milan to purchase books. This is not a code, it is a word game I made up to amuse myself on the train. The revolver? These are troubled times. When did I last see Carlo Cafiero and Andrea Costa? I do not know these men. I am a book trader.

If I fail to co-operate I will make it worse for myself. The insurrection is over. With respect, I inform him, I fear he has the wrong man. I know nothing of insurrection; further, I am completely extraneous to politics.

I am led out the door and down a corridor through a set of locked doors, and we pass a row of cells occupied by prisoners. At the end of the row, the guard leads me through another locked door and down a set of stairs into the row of isolation cells. He unlocks the first door and pushes me into the cell. All traces of light disappear when he slams the door.

The cell is damp, and I feel my way around to a wooden bench and I sit. My eyes slowly adjust to the dark and the black becomes shadows forming strange shapes in the space around me. I stand and walk the perimeter of the cell several times. There is nothing but the bench and the enterprise of human excrement.

■ ■ ■

I met Veronica about the time Vin took his first of three trips to Mexico, in the summer of 1989, to see old friends, meet new contacts and do research. I was coming out of the men's room at the Bradford Café in Central Square and she was going into the ladies' room. I already noticed her sitting at a table with a group of hippie-looking types and I gathered from eavesdropping they were activists of some kind. Light-headed from the draft beers I consumed with lunch at the Middle East, I passed the afternoon at the Bradford drinking seventy-five cent drafts. After the fourth or fifth time I looked, she asked me to join them.

She introduced herself and the rest of the dyed-in-the-wool hippies and younger kids who'd missed the 1960s experience but were hoping to recreate it in the 1980s. Veronica was in her early thirties, slightly overweight, pretty, long brown hair; in most ways the antithesis of what I was usually attracted to in a woman. The first thing I'd noticed was that she wore Birkenstock sandals. During the height of my bout with hippiedom in the late sixties I'd sworn off sandals, and over the years Birkenstocks had become some kind of symbol to me: I would rather run over a bed of nails shoeless than put a pair on my own feet. Her jeans were patched and her tank-top bared hairy armpits and through the scent of patchouli oil I detected her body odour.

She and her friends were working for the people living in Tent City on the back side of Central Square. Several streets lined with tenement houses were leveled and cleared for new office buildings and some ex-tenants who were put out, along with other Cambridge and Boston homeless, started a tent community on one of the lots. The city was trying to run them off but the local media picked up on the story, so city officials were treating the matter delicately. Two of the people in Veronica's group were lawyers, one of whom I knew. I first met Allen when he moved to Boston after living in a teepee in western Massachusetts for two years. We worked as waiters together until he went off to law school and I lost track of him. He still looked like a biker, which he wasn't: beard, earrings, hair down to his waist and tattoos. I listened to what they were saying about possible stays in city ordinances, about support from the local media coming just in time – but I knew it was in vain.

The following night Veronica and I met at the Willow for drinks. It was a neighborhood bar on Willow Avenue with an adjacent room where local and national musicians performed. The cover charge was cheap and so were the drinks. What a strange sensation it was to be in the bar side of the place each time the waitress opened the door and the sound of live jazz momentarily drowned the television set ever-tuned to a fight or a game. I should have seen the flags go up the minute Veronica said she liked jazz OK, but she liked all kinds of music; whatever was on the radio when she turned it on was fine. I asked her how long she'd known Allen and it turns out they'd dated but it was a thing of the past. We discussed the Tent City dilemma and I said no matter how strong you think your organization is, the old adage that you can't fight City Hall was true. I agreed with her about the state of social affairs but lost my urge to stand on line.

I had done a little in the late sixties and early seventies; but I was too busy working and trying to support myself after graduating high school. I moved out on my own within a month of graduating high school. Uncle Lenny, Aunt Rose and the greaser son were glad to see me go and I left without fanfare. I found a job working at a Sears Roebuck and Company store on Mass. Ave in Cambridge. I worked the loading dock five days a week and rented a one-bedroom apartment above Caputo's Pizza on Somerville Ave. I walked to work and kept to myself; in my off time my passion for reading and music consumed me. I borrowed books and records from the library and when I could I bought them. I had no plan or method of approaching things, I would listen to Phil Ochs, Beethoven, Miles Davis and the Beatles, I read any history book I could get my hands on and never knew if what I was reading was good or bad. I read it for the information it contained, every bit of which I thought I had to memorize and I was frustrated and felt stupid when I couldn't remember names, dates and events. I read Paul Goodman, who I heard speak at a church in Cambridge, Marx, Lao Tsu and Plato. Some of it I got. Much of it I didn't. Just try to get at the nature of it, my old high-school teacher would say. One thing just lead to another. On Sunday afternoon I walked to the Cambridge Commons to see rock concerts and girls.

Much went on outside my door with protests and student riots, the music and drugs. I tried to get involved in various local political movements but found them all tyrannical and stifling. At the same time, I was realizing that I didn't like people much and my best time was time spent alone. I tried pot for a while but it only made me agoraphobic and hungry. I preferred Southern Comfort. After two more years I grew tired of the loading dock and Sears and Roebuck's profit-sharing plan and left. I got a job as a short-order cook at a breakfast and lunch place on Mass. Ave between Harvard and Central Square. It was there I discovered life beyond 9 to 5. I worked three ten-hour shifts, five in the morning to three in the afternoon, with four days off. The owner paid me cash under the table and I quickly found that I had nearly doubled my free time and increased my cash intake.

I saw many bands perform at the Tea Party; the Modern Lovers on the Cambridge Commons; the New York Dolls at Jack's on Mass. Ave. I slept late. Read books. Ate meals alone and dreamed about having sex with women. With the exception of Aunt Rose, the only sex I knew was a week-long affair with a waitress from work who went back to her boyfriend then pretended it never happened. One day my old high-school teacher came in for lunch. I hadn't seen him in years. It was slow so we chatted. Mr Lepore wanted to know how I was getting along and asked had I thought about college? I barely made it through high school. It didn't matter. He said I was a smart kid, if I was interested he could help and he gave me his number.

That very day while walking home through Harvard Square I heard sirens and commotion as I neared the Commons, a wave of people were running towards me screaming and shouting, there was smoke, tear gas, people swarming and I was swept up with no choice but to turn and run or get mowed down. Later on the television they showed the riot in Harvard Square and students who occupied buildings and teachers speaking out on their behalf. Suddenly, the stuff I was reading in books and real life began to correspond. I phoned Mr Lepore and with his help I was enrolled in American History 101 as a part-time student at Boston State College.

Veronica loved the dogma of shoulds and should nots. She was a staunch vegetarian who preached at me while I devoured a bloody steak. She chided me for owning a car. People didn't need cars with public transportation. She hated television and blamed it for the problems of the world; and she had the habit of always steering conversations to things most important to her. I learned not to mind her hairy armpits and while her hairy legs put me off at first, I found them soft nonetheless. Perhaps I lost touch with my own values and passions, and lived vicariously through her. So we began to see each other, meeting for supper or attending bad political plays friends of hers wrote, produced and acted in. Physically, she wasn't as attractive as Carol. I felt comfortable not having to compete with her looks. Over the years I'd layered on a drinking belly which on my skinny frame looked sickly.

One afternoon I met Veronica at her apartment and she ran into my arms crying. Police squads moved in and cleared Tent City out by force. I held her tightly and tears soaked my shoulder.

October 1918

Carlo Valdinoci walks past expansive homes of celebrated Cambridge families. At the corner of Beacon Street he stops and looks up at the night sky, breathing in autumn's sweet decay.

It's been one year since he returned from Mexico. Three since he met Tina, when he was fully immersed in the movement, writing articles, making speeches, attending picnics. Her spirit and dedication equaled his own. She spoke and wrote in English, Italian; was fluent in Greek, Spanish and French. When she told Carlo of her plan to publish an anarchist paper in English he thought it a foolish idea, there wasn't enough interest in anarchism among the natives. But in no time *The Watchdog* circulation equaled any of the Russian, German, Italian or Jewish papers, much to the dismay of old-timers who had little faith in the non-immigrant faction.

He crosses Beacon on to Park. Cambridge tranquillity yields to Somerville's drone of factories second shift. Her last letter dated August 27 said still no news, any day now. He counts back the months certain he is the father.

At Somerville Avenue he turns right and walks the last blocks of tenements to Tina's flat. The avenue is quiet except for an occasional passing truck. Carlo climbs the three flights of stairs and down the rickety hall. He taps three times on the door. Three more. Footsteps across the hall, a bolt's unlocked, a tired face of an elderly woman peers from behind the door. There's no one there. Yes, she had a baby; it was a girl. She left in the middle of the night owing back rent.

He walks down through Union Square, turns and walks up Somerville Avenue again. At Central Street he turns right and ascends the hill, his breath vapors increase as he nears the crest. At the Highland Avenue intersection he turns toward City Hall and the new library, there he cuts down to Prospect Hill where the newly minted American flag was first flown in defiance of the British. A small fortress overlooked Cambridge, Charlestown, Boston, the Charles River, Boston Harbor and the Atlantic Ocean. Now a stone replica stands, erected while Carlo was in Mexico, the American flag flapping noisily overhead on a pole.

Carlo continues down the hill into a small wooded area and sits with his back against a tree. Night lights and sounds lay open one by one, the immediate surroundings and cities stretching out below. Animals rustle in nearby brush. Distant smokestacks billow into night-blue sky, rows of meat-packing plants lit from within. Two years, six days a week, ten hours a day he carried pig carcasses on his shoulder from the slaughtering area to the waiting meat hooks of the butchers. He places his hands in his pockets, wraps his coat tight around himself and closes his eyes.

from The Journals of Herbert Minderman:

We are victorious! Our determination has been effective and the workers and citizens once again freely speak their minds in Fresno. The prisoners have been released from jail and the I.W.W. has shown that passive resistance can ensure constitutional rights. We can act for ourselves and do so peaceably. Now we know that we have the strength to challenge the prevailing power. When the word reached our cell there were great cheers. Men slapped each other on the back and sang. I look out over the quiet street from my bedroom. To my dismay, my family and friends care little for our victory, only that I am safe and have returned home. The street is quiet. It is getting dark. Youngsters can be heard at play. Soon they will be called in for wash-up and bed time. When I was a boy I looked out at the neat houses in rows and heard the children yell their last thrills of the day and the sights and sounds brought me comfort. Now I feel distant from it all and alone.

Diary of Christina Donato:

'Fillipo finds a place for me in the attic of his brother's house. There is no heat, so I wear several layers of clothing and keep the baby wrapped in blankets. I sleep on a cot and there is a crib made out of a wooden box for Emma. She is either at my breast or asleep. I am under the spell of her tiny, pressed red face, her little frail hands, her fragile limbs and quiet cry. Day and night I am tired. Fillipo's brother's wife is a sturdy and generous woman. She brings me meals three times a day and sees to our needs. She and her husband believe that the baby belongs to Fillipo. Fillipo has finally accepted the fact that we are no longer lovers. He has taken care of me as his own, and I will never forget. One morning Carlo appears and is shown to the attic. He cries when he sees Emma and holds her so tight against him that he makes her cry. He says that we are a family now and urges me to come with him to his mother's farm. There we can remain until we find a way to Italy. My work is here I say, but he cannot understand. He says the Germans are on the verge of surrendering, when they do, the government will have more time and energy to focus on rounding up dissidents at home. It will mean jail for us all. This is all the more reason for me to remain; there is much work to be done. For several days Carlo visits me and our conversations follow the same path. He wants complete destruction through violent means of the old order, from the ground-level up, with no pre-planned organizing. I believe in restructuring from within, the general strike as non-violent means to an end and in bringing the government peacefully, if possible, to its knees. Syndicalized organizations are a necessary element in the new society. Violence has never, and will never bring constructive results. We must find new ways of envisioning the revolution to change the methods of revolution. Carlo places his head on his lap and cries that I cannot take his child from him. He has as much a right to her as I. But he knows,

as I do, that we cannot remain together, despite our love; we are too different and I will not be with any one man for the rest of my life. I am worried about him. His eyes are glazed and his thinking is fragmented. He has lost much weight and his cheeks are sunken. Galleani is captured and will be deported to Italy. Carlo says he will rest at his mother's farm, then go to New York where he can hide out. His last words after kissing me and the baby express that he is nearing the end of his rope.'

The Notebooks

'. . . November 11, 1887 – November 11, 1912! Twenty-five years, an infinitesimal fraction of time in the upward march of the race, but an eternity for him who dies many deaths in the course of his life. The twenty-fifth anniversary of the Chicago martyrdom intensified my feeling for the men I had never personally known, but who by their death had become the most decisive influence in my existence. The spirit of Parsons, Spies, Lingg, and their co-workers seemed to hover over me and give deeper meaning to the events that inspired my spiritual birth and growth . . . I stood erect before the dense mass of people. Its tense feeling mingled with mine, and all our hate and all our love were concentrated in my voice. "They are not dead," I cried; "they are not dead, the men we have come to honour tonight! Out of their quivering bodies dangling from the noose, new lives have emerged to take up the strains throttled on the scaffold. With a thousand voices they proclaim that our martyrs are not dead! . . ." Thus by 11 November 1918 the war was won, so far as arms could do it. Now came the great test of what kind of peace the Allies would impose and the Central Powers accept. For a "peace without victory" had long since been ruled out, even by President Wilson . . . The armistice was supposed to be in force for only sixty days . . . Actually, the Peace Conference did not even open for ten weeks, and peace-making required six months more

. . . During this time the Armistice was formally renewed monthly. And one of its severest terms, continuing the blockade until Germany signed a peace treaty, was relentlessly enforced, since the Allies wished to prevent a renewal of the war by Germany in case her government did not like the terms. This continued blockade caused more suffering in Germany than even the war, created dangerous bitterness, and fed that desire for revenge which Hitler later exploited . . . On November 11, at ten in the morning, the electric power in our shop was switched off, the machines stopped, and we were informed that there would be no further work that day. We were sent to our cells, and after lunch we were marched to the yard for recreation. It was an unheard-of event in the prison and everyone wondered what it could mean. My thoughts dwelt in the days of 1887. I had intended to strike against work on the anniversary that marked the birth of my social consciousness. But there were so few women able to go to the shop that I did not want to add to the number of absentees. The unexpected holiday gave me the opportunity to be alone for spiritual communion with my martyred Chicago comrades . . . Late in the evening the prison silence was torn by deafening noises coming from the male wing. The men were banging on bars, whistling, and shouting. The women grew nervous, and the block matron hastened over to reassure them. The declaration of armistice was being celebrated she said. What armistice? I asked. It's Armistice Day, she replied; that's why you have been given a holiday . . . Today the discovery of a computer virus affected computers at Harvard University, Boston University, and Charles University has university officials and experts suspecting sabotage. The virus affects computer memory by causing the memory base of a system to erase itself. In addition to the potential for the virus to delete every bit of information on a system's data base, the virus allows any hacker to easily seize control of computers running comparable programs and steal information on the machine's hard drive. One expert said that a slightly above average knowledge of computers would be needed to use the bug to wreak havoc since a simple command executed by exploiting the bug could wipe out or illegally copy volumes of data. State Police and the F.B.I. have been called in to help with the investigation . . .'

The Notebooks

'... Mr President ... To meet his menace of
socialism ... You should become the real leader
of the radical forces in America, and present to
the country a constructive program of
fundamental reform, which shall be an
alternative to the program presented by the
socialists, and the Bolsheveki ...'

■ ■ ■

Veronica was staying with me five or six nights a week by the time the country was gearing up for the Gulf War. She shared a crowded house with several room mates and we had more privacy at Vin's. Our sexual relations were on the wane, though it was easy when we were together, even when we frequently disagreed.

During the summer of 1990 the police raided the restaurant where I worked. The owner ran a gambling racket and laundered mob money. Large stashes of cash were found along with a set of books containing gambling and phony bookkeeping records. As soon as the owner was out on bail, he was up to his old tactics, taunting the police, who raided the establishment again while health inspectors cited the place for over two hundred violations. It was the third time that year the place had been cited, so the city shut the restaurant down.

For the first time in nearly ten years I had to look for a job. There was no way I could find a dishwashing job that paid like the old one so, against my preference, I took a waiter position at an upscale bistro in downtown Boston. The money was good, and I worked as few nights as possible to pay my rent and have a little spending cash. I continued with my habit of drinking and mooning around the apartment, working my way through Vin's library and micro-film archive, tens of thousands of pages of historic data, most of it never to make it to the history books.

Veronica and Vin got along well. Though they were opposed on many issues they didn't have the heightened tension of disagreement between lovers. Veronica worked at a shelter for homeless women. Her salary was slightly above minimum wage and the work was dangerous. Many women on the street had been released from institutions when the Reagan administration de-institutionalized health care. Those previously on medication to keep illnesses in check were now completely at the mercy of their diseases. Veronica had been scratched, punched, bitten, and spat upon. She held a master's degree and could have earned more in a safer setting.

She immediately became involved with anti-war activity and during her spare time organized marches and co-ordinated letter-writing campaigns. The local and national media was swept up in the anti-Iraq fervor. Saddam Hussein, the man who was Bush and Reagan's friend, whose military had been built up with U.S. subsidies, was now portrayed as the next Hitler and threat to the planet, with his army that was unable to defeat Iran during eight years of war.

The president stated that this would not be another Vietnam, which meant the country would fully commit itself and, contrary to what occurred in Vietnam, the media would not be free to bring the war home. The Gulf War was a Hollywood movie. Its plot unfolded each evening and millions viewed with the enthusiasm they showed during the Olympics. Combat footage video games.

That period was the nadir of my existence. Veronica was adamant about the importance of the anti-war campaign, but I had nothing to do with it. It was the final wedge that came between us. There was nothing any of us could do to change the course of history. All the letters written, all the marches, would have zero affect on the events. When the big anti-war march on Washington came, I refused to go with her. She accused me of being no better than the people waving yellow ribbons. The day she left for Washington I was sitting on the sofa, drinking beer and listening to Charlie Parker. You make me sick were her last words before walking out the door. She returned enthusiastically while I took delight in showing her the headlines from three major newspapers including *The New York Times*. The number of people present at the rally was reported on the first page of each of the publications with a difference of 200,000 amongst them. I told her you can't fight it it's too big.

Vin did little more than I in taking an active stance against the war, but Veronica was more tolerant of his inertia. Rather than argue with him, she listened as Vin talked the war out of the immediate, and placed it into a wider historical context, another inevitable event that civilization must go through.

'The fight for the control of oil in the Middle East has been ongoing since the end of World War I and probably won't be over until the last ounce of the fluid is pumped off. There's been an Iraqi democratic opposition to Saddam Hussein for years and most of the dissenters in exile in Europe find their pleas for support fall on deaf ears in Washington. And the connection between so-called Iraqi aggression and the problem of the Arab-Israeli conflict is hard to ignore – for twenty years presidents have claimed to be opposed to annexation and aggression while our administrations do nothing to stop Israeli annexations and armed aggression. Dear Veronica, this is a very complicated matter. It's not that I'm in favor of the war, but you shouldn't be so shocked or outraged that the country is at war again. Because of historical momentum, it's inevitable that we go to war again. In fact, I'd be shocked if we didn't. Especially in the Middle East. It's not simply a matter of black and white, but decades of shades of gray, here and abroad. And going out and marching against this war is like putting your finger through a hole in the dike while the rest of the island is already under water.'

The Gulf War didn't last long. One morning, Veronica and I woke and for a moment she poked about the messy bedroom. I asked her what she was looking for and she said her sandals. Before she'd spoken the words she tried to stop herself as if she instantly regretted having said them. I thought nothing of it until Veronica went into the shower and as I walked to the kitchen to put on a pot of coffee, something caught my eye from Vin's half-open bedroom door. Vin had gone out and I opened his door wide enough to see Veronica's Birkenstocks sitting on the floor by the bed. I said nothing about this when Veronica came out into the kitchen wearing her sandals. Veronica and I stopped making love during the war and I knew it was only a matter of time before the inevitable split. But Vin? He was at least old enough to be her father, and as long as I'd known him he appeared to have no sexual relationships.

I had to work a shift that night and when I came home Veronica was in bed and Vin was in his study working at his computer, a glass of grappa by his side. I walked in, intending to confront him, but I only managed to say hello. He said hello without looking up from the computer screen. As I left the room I detected the faint smell of patchouli oil.

I told Veronica of my discovery. She admitted that she and Vin had been lovers for several months. What was the big deal? she asked.

'He's my best friend and like a father to me. I would never sleep with your mother.'

'Believe me you wouldn't want to.'

'This isn't funny. The two of you betrayed me.'

'Don't make a bigger thing of it than it is.'

The Memoirs of Errico Malatesta, Early Years

In my youth being arrested and going to prison was part of my apprenticeship. The persecution only awakened my enthusiasm. But those early experiences were a joke compared with what would happen later.

There was always work to do in prison. I brought the word to prisoners and guards alike; only a fine line separates the two. The anarchist's struggle is not much different from both their struggles. We all must eat. The man who opposes the law in order to feed and clothe his family, is not dissimilar from the man who takes a job to uphold the law, who also wants to care for his family. They are poor devils from the same background.

It is a curious thing to watch, when I speak to a convict or a guard about developing brotherly feelings and mutual respect. There is something about those words that unsettles them so. But respect and the desire for the well-being of others must enter into the customs and manifest themselves not as duties, but as a normal element of social instincts. This cannot be done by force. I do not believe in the infallibility, nor even the general goodness of the masses. But I believe even less in the infallibility and goodness of those who hold power and legislate, even less in those in charge of policing.

Some have accused me of cowardice, of running away instead of taking responsibility for my actions. As I matured, I learned to take more calculated risks. There have been times when my serving time in prison has been in the best interest of the cause. There have also been times when I could do more effective work in another country. When it became impossible for me to do anarchist propaganda in Italy, I lived elsewhere. I am a man with a cause. I am not a hero.

Sept. 11, 1918

Dearest Tina,

By the time you receive this letter, it will be over. Perhaps, my words will serve you and our child as a measurement of the purity of my motives. I can not expect you to approve; but, I do want to earn your respect. I can see only the act now; and I have made a clear choice. I believe the most noble thing a true revolutionary can do is remove a tyrant. As sacred as human life is, the tyrant is the enemy of the people and the killing of a tyrant is not murder. I would never commit murder. The killing of a tyrant is an act of liberation; it breathes life into oppressed people. It is an act of love on the part of the revolutionary, one which he takes on in spite of the fact that the act itself may cost him his own life. To give of oneself is truly the ultimate sacrifice of the revolutionary. It is impossible to separate such an individual act of rebellion from the political climate in which it strikes; from the various causes, in their complexities, near and far, that determine such an act; from the consequences and the impact such an act imprints on our minds and experience. The church and state despise such acts. The latter defines anyone who breaks any law as a criminal and will deliver him to jail or the executioner. The former will sentence him to hell. But, historically, what two institutions have been responsible for more violence, more bloodshed, more injustices upon the human race than the church and state? They cry out that human life is inviolable while they get richer condemning men to toil in the fields, factories and mines, women to prostitution, children to the gutters. Or they force the young men on to battlefields for the sake of gold or the stock market. I know you will say, 'When one tyrant dies, another will take his place,' and that any attempt to end the life of a tyrant is futile. Even among the ranks of anarchists there are those who believe that acts of violence will only bring stronger repression, and that the true way of progress is through slow, persistent propaganda, organization and preparation. But you too easily separate the individual act of rebellion from the revolutionary process of which the individual act is an essential and initial phase. The individual act of rebellion leads to the first heroic, if often doomed insurrections; these will be followed by future triumphs through other revolutionary deeds. The individual act of rebellion is a necessary intermediary act between the ideal or theoretical, and the insurrectionary movement which follows. It sparks the fire of the revolution. It is impossible for the revolutionary to reject or condemn the individual act of rebellion. It is no more possible to reject an earthquake, flood, or any other natural disaster. We can only endure such phenomena which arise from causes beyond the power of mankind. The journalists of the ruling class are bought and paid for; the police and their informers and the cowardly magistrates will always have the public believe that such individual acts originate from plots. On the contrary, such individual acts almost always rise from one individual's conscience and the impulse to perform the utmost deed for the future of humanity. Further, the journalists and officials would have the masses believe that such individuals are degenerates and idiots. The truth is, those who have attacked the church and state in the past have risen from oppression and suffering, and are the foremost in normality, education and intelligence. Historically, countless episodes of barbarous ferocity have been inflicted upon the world's poor and downtrodden masses. This has been the case in Europe, Russia, and in these United States, which, only sixty years ago, allowed the enslaving of human beings, and still allows the public lynching of negroes. With all the bloodshed, violence and horror inflicted upon the people by the keepers of tyranny, why should one single act of violence by one individual acting out in his fullest conscience against tyranny seem so appalling? The poets have long been celebrated for their courageous denouncements against tyranny in the name of justice and humanity. Their words have been canonized, arousing compassion and ardor for the fallen rebel, and the ideal that inspired the rebellion. Many dream of the day that a revolution will break out and once and for all end the long feud between the oppressors and the oppressed. But, too often, these well-wishers look upon that day in some far off future, in another time and place. We must start the revolution from within ourselves and throw away all of the old superstitions, self-imposed ignorance, foolish vanities and moral deficiencies. Being children of the bourgeois regime, it is near impossible to discard its bestial shackles. But we are revolutionary only when we are able to resist and react against the immorality, vice and violence of our environment. The individual act by deed can incite moral exaltation and freedom, like a stone cast into a pond, the ripples widening farther and farther away from the stone's point of entry. Remember, the individual act of rebellion is caused by a long series of predisposing conditions; and there are no fruitless or harmful acts of rebellion. Every act has deep echoes and resonance which compensate for it. This is not nostalgia for needless savageness. It would be preferred that every act of rebellion had such a sense of proportion that its consequences correspond to its cause. Unfortunately, the individual act of rebellion, due to intrinsic and extrinsic causes, the moment in time in which it is undertaken, the environment and the circumstances of the act, cannot be different from what it is. Its effect may be immediate, or its nobility and chivalry might impact only the future generations. But make no mistake, each act fights cowardice and oppression, rebels against submission, teaches us, and does the work of revolution. History has proven the futility of hopes in legal means of resistance for progress and success. All of our papers, pamphlets, marches, petitions, meetings, lectures, councils, votes, parliamentary victories, searching for the right leaders – have they unlocked the chains that shackle the proletariat? We have exhausted the legal means for change and now pay the price with humiliation and wounds. Every social advancement has resulted from difficult struggle and uprisings. Do you think that the holders of all the wealth and power along with their appointed authorities will have a change of heart and behave differently? All the disagreements between organizationalists and individualists of anarchism are trivial in comparison to the magnitude of the task at hand and our ultimate goals. The first step on the way to revolution is the individual act of rebellion. It is inseparable from propaganda, from the mental groundwork which precedes revolution, integrates it, leads to larger, future, collective insurrections which will flow into the social revolution. No act of rebellion is ineffectual. No act of rebellion is damaging. All acts of rebellion are acts of love.

All my love, for ever
Carlo

from The Journals of Herbert Minderman, 1914:

My cell mates speak their native languages and what a confusion with the Greeks, Italians and Serbs talking all at once. Only two men speak English. Claus, a gentle Swede from Michigan, and Victor, who is the son of an ex-slave from Mississippi. Word from the outside is the national guard fired upon striking miners with machine guns and killed twenty-five miners, many of them were women and children who burned to death when the guardsmen set fires to disperse the miners and their families from the tent colony. Our first response in the cells was a non-stop battleship. The guards and the sheriff came but their clubs were ineffective. The more they beat us, the stronger our agitation. We kept up the battleship until six in the morning. Then we made a silent vigil in memory of the victims of the Ludlow Massacre. No one in the cell spoke a word until six in the evening. We are on rations of bread and water. But we will not eat or drink for three days in memory of the victims. My thoughts are with Mother Jones. Her recent speech inspired us all but her whereabouts has been unknown since she was arrested. There has been a call to arms by the United Mine Workers. All over Colorado strikers are preparing for battle. Several divisions of National Guardsman have been stranded at railroad stations because railroad workers would not take them to the trouble areas. One troop of army regulars refused to take part in action against the miners who are up in arms all over the Ludlow area. The regulars say they will not engage in the shooting of innocent women and children. Around the country there are demonstrations against what has happened. There are pickets in front of Rockefeller's office in New York City. Colorado's governor has asked for federal troops to restore order. One cell mate said if there's going to be a civil war then let it begin over the Ludlow Massacre.

The Notebooks

'... The Times had referred to Mexico. On the morning that the bodies were discovered in the tent pit at Ludlow, American warships were attacking Vera Cruz, a city on the coast of Mexico – bombarding it, occupying it, leaving a hundred Mexicans dead – because Mexico had arrested American sailors and refused to apologize to the United States with a twenty-one-gun salute. Could patriotic fervor and the military spirit cover up class struggle? Unemployment, hard times, were growing in 1914. Could guns divert the attention and create some national consensus against an external enemy? It surely was a coincidence – the bombardment of Vera Cruz, the attack on the Ludlow colony. Or perhaps it was, as someone once described human history, "the natural selection of accidents". Perhaps the affair in Mexico was an instinctual response of the system for its own survival, to create a unity of fighting purpose among a people torn by internal conflict. The bombardment of Vera Cruz was a small incident. But in four months the First World War would begin in Europe...'

■ ■ ■

I moved out of Vin's within days. A co-worker shared a large house with others where a tiny bedroom was available for one hundred dollars a month. Without a word to Vin or Veronica, I gathered my things and left. My new room was a walk-in closet, no space to walk around the mattress with the stereo, records, tapes and books stacked up the wall. I kept my clothes in a duffel bag, and entering my room meant falling on to the mattress where any interaction in the room had to take place. I was glad it was over with Veronica; but losing Vin shook me.

I was forty-three years old. Everything I owned I packed up into my old Chevy. Except for Vin, I had no close friends; nor did I have any living relatives I wanted to see. For ten years I was a part-time dishwasher with yards of free time on my hands and little to show for it. I read books, listened to music, drank too much and screwed up a good relationship while people I went to college with established themselves and raised children. My imagination flashed on the man that Vin and I passed that morning on Tremont Street in the South End. I wondered which of us lived the fool's life.

When I was a kid and my mother was alive two of her cousins came to live with us. Alberto was married and hoped to make enough money to bring his family over; Gianni was single, still a teenager. My parents rented them the upstairs flat for a nominal fee, and the two men worked as bricklayers for a year saving every penny until they decided to return to Italy. They hated America, and missed their farm. More than once Alberto broke up fights between my mother and father. One time my father hit me and my mother Alberto threatened that if he ever raised a hand to either of us again, he would be sorry. My father was many things, but not a fighter. The period of time Gianni and Alberto lived upstairs was the most peaceful of my childhood. Since my mother died, I'd heard nothing about them. I wasn't sure if they were alive.

I worked as many shifts as I could at the bistro. Six and seven days per week, lunch and dinner shifts; in six months I saved ten thousand dollars. I took my meals at work and slept through my days off.

One night Vin appeared when I was cleaning up from a shift. He said it was time we talked. I finished and we drank at a local bar. It was awkward. Long silences and small talk. I didn't know how to break in.

'Jesus fucking Christ, Vin, how could you?'

'Gregorio, what do you mean how could I? How can you ask me such a question? Does it seem so out of the realm of possibility? You told me many a time while she was with you that you didn't see it working out.'

'That doesn't mean you turn around and fuck your friend's girlfriend.'

'*Girlfriend*. Alas, I've never heard you use such a word before. I thought you always referred to them as *women*. And besides, she consented to it. It wasn't as if we plotted behind your back. It just happened. It was gradual. There's more hidden in a cause than what can readily be seen in the effect. One evening we just found ourselves in bed together.'

'There doesn't have to be a plot, Vin. And things don't necessarily *happen* on their own. Sometimes people *let* things happen.'

'What difference does it make if things happen, or you let them happen? The fact is things like this happen. And besides, you talk about the virtues of free love. It's not cheating, it's just sex. One of life's greatest pleasures. Who's to say any of us owns the rights to anyone else's sex.'

'I'm not. It's just when it's so close to home, it hurts. I can't believe you can't understand that. Christ, you've been like a father to me and then you turn around and sleep with my lover.'

'I must say, from what the both of you told me it wasn't as if the two of you were hot and heavy.'

'Oh is that right? Well what the fuck else did she tell you? Did she compare the size of our cocks?'

'Gregorio, Gregorio. You're losing your perspective on things.'

'Jesus, Vin, what do you expect? Don't you understand? With the exception of Carol, you're the only person in my adult life who has mattered to me.'

'All the more reason not to let the situation come between us.'

We closed one bar and moved on to another, never coming to any understanding or resolution, two tennis players taking our swings. As the night wore on we tired of the debate, and at an all-night breakfast joint over eggs and bacon, I sloppily told Vin my plan to go to Italy. He liked the idea. There were many contacts there and he could put me in touch with them. By the time we left the eatery it was as if we were friends again and we parted with a hug at first light.

When I woke I was still angry; and I continued to keep my distance from Vin. He called the bistro several times but I avoided his efforts to meet with excuses. A few days before I departed for Italy, he phoned to say he had a list of contacts for me to look up and packages he wanted me to mail for him when I got there. I left without meeting him or saying good-bye.

The Notebooks

'. . . In part of a nationwide movement to round up anarchists under the Anti-Anarchist law, yesterday Department of Justice agents and area police raided over a dozen homes and cities. Twenty-one people were arrested. In Somerville, a printing press was located inside a stable off Park Street . . . A spokesman for the police said that authorities have been aware of the press in the area for several months and, despite efforts, were unable to determine its whereabouts. The difficulties were made clear at the time of the raid: the press was portable. It was installed on the bed of a truck so that it could be moved from location to location. Authorities believe that for several years this press has been responsible for printing anarchist literature, including an anarchist newsletter called *The Watchdog*. Several people known to be involved with the press are still at large, including *The Watchdog's* publishers Rossa Nero and Fillipo Brusa of Somerville. Both names are believed to be aliases . . . Hundreds of dissidents all over the country, most of them immigrants from Europe and Russia, have been arrested in the past month under the Anti-Anarchist law. Dozens of meeting places and presses have been raided and literature and correspondence confiscated. Those arrested and found guilty face immediate deportation to their native countries. In a public statement made last evening, Attorney General Mitchell Palmer said, "This is only the beginning." The Attorney General made it clear that, with the Great War behind us and victory on our side, the United States will no longer stand idle and allow foreign dissent to undermine American ideals of freedom and democracy . . .'

Bentham, Massachusetts, 1919

'I was six when my father brought the family here. There were many assassinations in Europe during the 1890s, and many of them done by Italian anarchists. The pressure was mounting at home, and my father thought that in order to continue to propagate his ideals it would be best to leave Italy since he'd twice been jailed for his activities there. He planned to take us to Cecilia Colony in Brazil, my uncle was one of the colony's founders. But shortly before we were to depart, my uncle wrote that the colony was disintegrating and he was moving to New York City. So my father changed his plans and we sailed for America. It took everything we had to get here. All we brought with us were the belongings in our trunks. My uncle found us a flat, and secured work for my father and brother as construction laborers. It wasn't long before my father and uncle began working with the other Italian immigrants in New York City, carrying on with revolution. My father and uncle were well read, though they never had a formal education. My brother and I were taken to local meetings of the Italian anarchists. Books on every subject were passed amongst members of the groups. Meetings were held in little storefronts or back rooms of saloons, and speakers talked about the revolution, oppression, the evils of government and capitalism and how the masses would some day rise up and take what was rightly theirs.

'There was much poverty around. But it's funny, when all you know is one thing, it's hard to compare it with anything else. I don't remember those times as being poor. Most of the men in the neighborhood worked, but there never seemed to be enough money to secure everything that a family needed. My father and brother worked six days a week and ten hours a day and there were times when all we ate was broth and bread. Our clothes were in a constant state of disrepair and my mother did everything she could to keep them mended. It was a two-room flat. My brother and I slept in the front room, which was used as a living room by day. There was a tiny pantry which my mother made to function as a kitchen. Our bathing was done with the use of a wash tub in the pantry, which we closed off with curtain for privacy. We froze during winter and sweated through summer with only one small window in the front room allowing very little ventilation. On Sundays we attended the outdoor picnics where there was plenty of food to go around. All of the women cooked and the men brought their wine. After the meals there was music and singing and fiery speeches by the men. Of course when I was young the politics meant little to me.

'Two things happened when I was fourteen that turned my life around. There was an accident. A wall under construction caved in and my father and brother were buried beneath it along with two other men. They died instantly. My father and brother's death devastated my mother. She never wanted to come here and had no concern whatsoever for politics. She went silent. Finally it was proposed by my uncle that my mother and I return to Italy. Her family was there and we could live with her sister.

'Arrangements were being made to send us back to Italy, when one night my uncle took me to a meeting at a theater. It was a big gathering for anarchists and socialists in New York, a celebration of Emma Goldman's release from prison where she served time for advocating birth control. Maria Rodda was only sixteen years old and had recently arrived from France where she was in prison for two years. In Europe she was the member of an anarchist group headed by Santa Caserio when she was only fourteen. Caserio was the man who killed France's president Sadi Carnot. She was a beautiful young woman with long black curly hair and dark eyes that burned. Only two years older than I, it seemed like there were decades of experience between us. She spoke eloquently in a high-pitched voice about the evils of persecution in America, and countries like Italy and France; when she was finished, even those in the audience who spoke no Italian were aroused. I wanted so much to trade places with her, to have the badge of two years' imprisonment to hold the adulation of a theater full of people – to have been a comrade of someone who killed a tyrant. After Maria Rodda, Emma Goldman came out and spoke about birth control, workers' rights and free speech. Her words struck out loudly to every corner of the hall. Until that time, at the picnics and local store-front meetings the speakers had always been men speaking to men. The women in the movement were always relegated to preparing the food and caretaking of the children. Here in front of me were two women who brought the full house to the edge of its seats. Somehow I knew that what these women said related to the deaths of my father and brother. I left the hall knowing what my life was going to be.'

The baby began to stir in Giulia's arms. 'She's hungry,' she said, handing Emma over to Tina, who opened her blouse and put the baby to her nipple. Tina continued.

'I pleaded with my uncle to let me remain in America. I was willing to work for the movement at any cost. If I returned to Italy I would be doomed to a life of drudgery in a small village, married off and silenced. It was already known that I was a gifted writer for a girl of my age, and the fact that I could speak and write in Italian and English was in my favor. Most of the work my uncle was doing was within the Italian-speaking community. Their newspaper was in Italian, but they urgently needed someone who could read and translate from English in order to keep up with the mainstream papers and other English-written socialist literature. The main problem would be to convince my mother. Sadly, this was solved when she took sick. Her lungs filled up with fluid and she died on Christmas Eve. As with the death of my father and brother, I don't remember her death as being catastrophic for me; though as the years have worn on have I grown to miss and grieve for all of them. Especially my mother. My uncle and aunt took me into their family and loved me as if I was their own child.

"The years following my mother's death I worked for my uncle's newspaper, helped organize meetings, and with the immense library made available to me through the community, I read philosophy, science, and literature. Besides all the books and anarchist propaganda I devoured, in the neighborhoods I saw first hand the poverty of the immigrants and poor natives – men and women who were predestined to a life of drugs, prostitution, improper medical care, insufficient wages, inadequate housing and clothing, malnutrition and life-claiming diseases.

'I met Carlo at one of the anarchist picnics when I was twenty. There were several speakers that day, including Carlo. I was instantly attracted to his looks, and to his dedication to the cause. And that afternoon we talked with each other and it was as if we were of one mind. It was partly the enthusiasm of youth, of course, because in time, Carlo and I took different approaches in our methods. But we fell in love and I followed him to Boston and became involved with the East Boston Group there. Carlo and I almost married. Instead, he went off to Mexico.

'I'll find him in New York. He has urged me to go to Italy with him. I've resisted up to now, but everything is changing. I appreciate you having us; I know how your husband feels about us being here. These last few days have allowed us much needed rest. Tomorrow I will leave for New York. When I find Carlo, we will find a way to return to Italy. Perhaps the climate is right for us there.'

Emma finished feeding and Tina buttoned her blouse. She shifted the baby in her arms to cradle her.

Giulia stared at mother and child and said, 'I want you to know that I am proud of you all.'

New York City, February 1919

The train is late but Carlo Valdinoci is patient. Dressed in borrowed flannel suit, hair combed, clean-shaven, bushy mustache trimmed down, hazel green eyes clear, he steps aboard the train, takes his seat and slides his brown leather suitcase under it. A gray-haired businessman sits next to him, immediately opens his briefcase, removes papers and begins to work. The last travelers settle in and the engineer wrenches the whistle. Scratchy words over the loud speaker. Carlo sits up. The train lurches forward, hustle of people along the platform, was it Tina laden with bags and baby? They will understand him in time. The conductor sleepily collects tickets. Carlo stares out the window, the train stretches into night, New York City lights crisscross the window. Carlo feels light inside. Warm tones pumping blood.

■■■

Within hours of landing in Naples, I was sitting in cousin Alberto's kitchen enjoying a cup of espresso with Maria. I had started out from Naples with the bay on one side and Mt Vesuvius on the other. There were several bus changes to negotiate and each bus snaked higher into the hills. Open windows couldn't alleviate heat from the afternoon sun suffocating the landscape. I was thirsty and scared. What if I didn't remember the town correctly? What if they don't live in the town any longer? What if they're dead and gone? The bus rolled onward and upward when, after a long steep climb and hairpin turn, it came to a halt in the middle of a village and the driver told me this was San Sossio.

I stood in the middle of the road and watched the bus disappear into the hills, its gear-shifts fading out of ear-shot. There was a bar, a little gas station, and several older men sitting on public benches staring at me. In my rough Italian I asked if any one knew Alberto or Gianni Gilberto, and a fountain erupted, each of them talked excitedly waving their hands. A young boy ran off and returned with a square-jawed, stout woman of about sixty years with cropped gray hair, in a plain blue dress and darker blue apron. I told her who I was.

'Gregorio,' she shrieked, and took my face between her hands to kiss me. She motioned for me to follow her and insisted on carrying my bag despite my attempts to wrestle it from her. By this time villagers gathered and followed us curiously. Maria told them I was an American. My college Italian clashed with the dialect I learned from my parents, and the rapid-fire manner of speech I heard since landing in Naples was beyond my grasp. I could only catch a word or short phrase.

Alberto's wife Maria said Alberto was at the farm with Gianni and would soon return and be excited to see me. I had no plan, but enough money for a few months traveling if I slept and ate inexpensively. I also left a few thousand dollars in an account at home for when I returned. She sat at the kitchen window crocheting and I sat at the table. The kitchen floor was inlaid with intricate tile and an open hearth fireplace was used for some of the cooking, and heat during the winter. Maria used her new electric stove and oven sparingly, her first. On the counter a portable television was always switched on to overdubbed American television shows or Alberto's beloved soccer games.

We conversed as best we could that afternoon as I made frequent consultations with my portable dictionary and she chuckled each time. Eventually, a car with a leaky exhaust pulled up and she said it was Alberto. He walked into the kitchen, recognized me immediately and wrapped his arms around me. When the tears dried, he disappeared and returned with several bottles of wine. In English he said, You and me drink all this tonight.

Over a supper of hearth-grilled sausages and roasted peppers, Alberto said there was plenty of work at harvest time. I could remain as long as I wished and earn keep by helping out on the farm. Alberto's olive grove was on the edge of the village and on it stood a shack. Alberto offered me the shack, or, if I preferred, I could live with them in their house, there were two extra rooms and I was welcome.

The shack was a single-room stucco job with a terra cotta roof, nestled on a sun-exposed hill surrounded by the olive grove. The bed was steel spring, the water pumped ice cold and a bottled gas lamp hung over a two-burner gas stove. Mice had overrun the place and it took me several days to clean. Maria lent me basics such as an espresso pot, towels and bed-makings.

The first days in San Sossio I met and took meals with my mother's various cousins. All of the women cooked exquisitely and the men made wine, each with their own idiosyncrasies.

There were old-timers who remembered my mother as a girl and spoke fondly of her. Across the road from a public fountain where women once did laundry by hand, a little house my mother lived in as a child was still standing. One of my newly discovered cousins took me to his farm and pointed out a root cellar where my mother frequently hid when she was a girl.

I never knew such privacy and contentment as living in that shack. Mornings I rose to espresso and biscotti, which I took at a wooden table by an open window looking out on to a valley of crops, with olives, grapes and herbs wafting in the air. Alberto picked me up at 6:00 A.M. and drove the short distance to the farm. Alberto and Gianni's children, like most of the others of the current generation of young adults in the village, had married and gone off to the cities. During my first days in San Sossio, it was clear that the older people, and some young children, were very much present; but people my age either left town or worked outside of it. Alberto and Gianni were the last generation who would work the land. Alberto's son was a dentist in Naples, his daughter had married a factory worker and lived in Milan. Alberto and Gianni had no idea what would become of their farm after they were gone. The only groceries I saw them purchase were bread from the village's wood-burning oven bakery, coffee, milk, or cheese made by local cheese makers.

The brothers had aged physically since I'd seen them over three decades before. Alberto was now in his early sixties but, as I remembered from my youth, he worked with the strength of two young men. He chain-smoked cigarettes and constantly coughed but his body was like granite. His day began with a cup of espresso, a shot of whisky, and a cigarette. There were tomatoes, olives, apples, pears, figs, melons, herbs, cherries, eggplant, squash, potatoes, and peppers to be tended and picked. The chickens and pigs needed daily feeding and their coops and pens required cleaning. Produce we harvested was brought to Maria, and Gianni's wife, Felice, who jarred, pickled, and lined the shelves of their pantries. Chickens were killed and eaten as necessary, pigs were slaughtered according to needs and the meat cured, sausages preserved in olive oil, and even the knuckles and skin salt-cured and later simmered in tomato sauces. They made the most fruity olive oil and Alberto's wine was considered to be the finest in the village.

It took several weeks before my blisters healed and my backache abated. I was welcome to bathe at Alberto and Maria's, but they fully bathed once a week. I didn't want to overstep my bounds and did the same. I ate with Alberto and Maria, and sometimes Gianni and Felice. Some days we returned from the farm for a grand lunch, and dinner was light. Other days we brought sandwiches, worked through late afternoon and ate lavish dinners.

My night walks back to the shack were the perfect moments of the day. I stopped at the bar for a whiskey, fluent enough in the language for chat and gossip with locals. Then I walked home on the back road, smoking, staring up at the brilliant sky above a blinky San Sossio. At the shack I washed with cold water and collapsed into bed; consumed by silence and the day's work I slept in depths I'd never known previous.

I grew close to my cousins. As time passed we had discussions over meals on the simplest matters to world politics. They seemed no more or less informed and full of prejudices than people at home, and when it came to politics they had a special cynicism. Alberto said that he'd lived through over forty governments since Mussolini, and his life never changed one bit from government to government. He believed government had nothing to do with the little people, and was only for the rich to help them manage their money. Besides, when the Americans left the Mafia in place after World War Two, Italy wasn't liberated but doomed. Gianni and Alberto didn't understand how so many different kinds of people lived in America. Gianni believed that was the problem with America – too many different kinds of people and, with all of those differences, people only cared about their own interests.

In October the weather began to cool at night and the temperature dipped. I made use of the small woodstove and it kept me warm as long as I woke every two hours to refill it. By early November everything was harvested and preserved. Alberto and Gianni made enough wine to fill four hundred bottles. In the old days, this was the time for them to go to the north or leave the country for a few months where they worked construction to earn extra cash.

One day Alberto drove us out to a picnic in the countryside at the ruins of an old estate called the Castle of the Wind. Alberto said in the past, it was a meeting place for revolutionaries and bandits, and it was rumored a large stash of loot was buried on the grounds. Over the years many people had searched for the loot but never found anything, though someone once dug up several cases of rifles. On our way home Alberto drove to the top of the mountain above San Sossio. At a sharp turn in the road he pulled over and motioned for us to get out. I could see valleys and villages stretching out toward the Mediterranean. On this very spot Alberto told me, pointing to the edge of a long drop-off, a great-great uncle of mine died when his wagon turned over and tumbled down the hill. His widow married a fish merchant and moved to America.

Harvest time over, I was welcome to stay as long as I wanted. I decided I'd take some time away from San Sossio and travel. I still had most of the money I arrived with, and purchased a rail pass. Over the next six weeks I visited Naples, Pompeii, Rome, Florence, Venice, Padova and Milan, staying at inexpensive pensiones and eating delectable wine-drenched meals at little trattorias. I walked mazes of streets, visited museums and churches, drank hundreds of divine espressos laced with anisette at as many different bars, no two espressos ever the same.

My mother was much on my mind. Being in San Sossio allowed me to see her in a fresh context and knowing that she experienced a healthy and happy childhood comforted me. There were times when I forgot what she looked like, and I would remove the only photo I kept of her from my wallet and study it to recognize her again.

One night in Milan I was walking down a street and made eye contact with an elderly streetwalker. Something between my legs stirred. It was a year since I experienced any physical contact with a woman. I thought I must have been mistaken, but when I turned, she turned too. In the haze of sex, I knew that people had peculiar tastes. Perhaps she was a madam. Moreover, she resembled my aunt Rose. Or what my aunt Rose might look like now. I hadn't seen her in years.

I lived with my father for a year or so after my mother died. Then he lost the house and left me with aunt Rose and uncle Lenny. Uncle Lenny was really his half-brother. After my grandfather died a premature death, my grandmother married again, an American, and gave birth to Lenny with my stepgrandfather. My four grandparents were dead as long as I could remember. I learned about them through hearsay and a few family photographs. My father was around for two or three years. I'd see him after school, or he took me to a hockey game or wrestling match at the Boston Garden. Then I never saw him again. I heard he moved to Las Vegas, and, later, California.

Rose and Lenny weren't married. Rose was older than Lenny and had a son. Joe was a brute who graduated from vocational school the year I moved in. He worked at an auto parts store, drove a hot rod, his arms were tattooed and his hair slicked back. Joe had no interest in me, and I can't remember more than a two-sentence conversation with him. Later I heard he died in a car accident when his car went off the highway and into a house.

Lenny paid me little mind, though Rose, sometimes, could be very nice. But I never knew what kind of mood she would be in. It could change overnight. There were times when she was loving, as if I were her own, and she took time to talk with me about school, or ask why I didn't go out with other kids or play sports. Sometimes she took me to the North End for a pizza. Rose knew everyone. She made her drop-off at a tiny basement grocery and sandwich store run by a woman named Anna who would make me a salami sandwich to take home. When she wasn't happy Rose was silent, withdrawn, and she would act cruelly at the slightest annoyance. One time she stayed up for a week cleaning and recleaning the apartment, closets and floors, pantries and drawers, talking excessively about things that didn't make sense. Lenny tried to get her to eat or sleep but she paid him no mind. Finally, he brought her to the hospital where she remained for several weeks.

They lived above a grocery store and kept book. Uncle Lenny worked construction at one time but had a friend smack him in the face with a two-by-four and claimed some planks fell on him from above so he collected a monthly disability with a permanent scar on his face. One of them was always on the phone, there were piles of cash around, and men and women came and went. Joe refused to let me move into his room, so Lenny and Rose gave me the only extra space in the house, a tiny den. The room was doorless, though eventually they put up a plastic sliding thing. Since the den was right off the kitchen where Lenny and Rose conducted business, I went to sleep and woke to the ringing phone and strangers. Though they never said so, I know they resented me, especially as time wore on and my father stopped sending money.

Rose tried to make sure there was food around; I did my own laundry, managed to get myself off to school in the morning, and stayed out of the way. When the weather was good I played in the small yard, watching trucks make deliveries to the grocery store. The old man who owned the grocery store's name was Benny and he had a sad old dog with bloodshot eyes who moped around the creaky wooden floor of the store. Colder months I hung out inside Benny's or remained in my room and listened to my transistor radio. As I grew older, I began to read and went to the library. Lenny and Rose said if I read too many books I would hurt my head.

Rose wore lots of make-up and her blouses and sweaters tight.

Through openings between buttons I eyed her fleshy bra and fantasized about her oversize breasts. She wasn't pretty the way I remembered my mother to be, and she carried extra weight. But there was something about the way she swore, or stuffed her cigarettes out in her naked-woman ceramic ashtray and butts accumulated with her red lipstick around tips of white filters. When she came into my room that day, she knew what I was doing under the covers because she spied on me before. She sat on the edge of the bed smiling, she took my left hand, placed it on her breast and reached under the blanket.

I grew dizzy and sat on the edge of the sidewalk, head between my knees. I was an ocean away from home, alone as the day my mother was buried. I walked out on the only woman I ever loved because somewhere I convinced myself that nothing was worth the effort. My values like morality, ethics, remaining true to my dreams, had not inspired real action or commitment. On the farm I worked hard, I ate hearty and slept soundly, the world spun without the slightest consideration for me. My face weathered and dirt lodged under my fingernails. The night sky over San Sossio grounded me to a life I could live before dying. But it was not my life. Then I remembered what my cousin said about the wagon overturning and my great great uncle dying and his wife marrying a fish merchant and moving to America. And I remembered the various bits and pieces of information Vin had offered about his past, and facts I had already been putting together from my research in Vin's archives before I moved out. Vin's great grandparents were my great great uncle and aunt.

I paid a woman to be with me that night, and the following morning took a train. It was December. The train came out of a tunnel somewhere below Milan in a whirling snow storm. I couldn't see out of the window, my thoughts raced. My hands in dirt grabbing wild mushrooms, chasing chickens, walking the ruins of Pompeii, pigs running for their lives, picking olives and tomatoes, a bar on a Roman street, sitting at the wooden table in my shack on the hillside, the art of Florence and dizzying height of Giotto's tower which I couldn't finish climbing because my fear of heights, Giulia's loving dinners and the hills around San Sossio, the canals of Venice and a bad band at Saint Mark's Square, blood spurting in heartbeats from a chicken's throat, the candle-light blaze inside the Duomo of Milan, the noisy clothes-lined chaos of Naples and the smell of a woman on my newly grown mustache.

I would spend the holidays with my cousins and leave in January. I didn't have to return to the stifling nature of the university; whatever I needed access to, I could get from Vin. I would take up my studies in earnest and write a book. When I met a good woman, I would not let her go.

The Notebooks

'. . . After the years of frustration in London during the 1914-1918 war, Malatesta, after much difficulty, managed to return to Italy at the end of 1919, and the next three years (apart from the period of ten months in prison) were probably among the most active and rewarding in his long lifetime, even though once again the hoped-for insurrection did not materialise, and the defeat of the working-class movement in Italy was to be marked by Mussolini's "march" to power. As well as editing daily anarchist paper *Umanità Nova*, Malatesta addressed meetings all over Italy, and was engaged in seeking to bring together all the revolutionary elements in the Socialist and Republican parties, and in the trade union movement. A detailed study of this period would be a rewarding task for it would not only give a clear picture of Malatesta at work and his method of working, but also show to what extent a movement without large resources, and including in its ranks all shades of anarchism, including anti-organisers and believers in organisation, could work together for a common cause . . . Malatesta, however, warned that the new government had been set up in Russia "above the Revolution in order to bridle it and subject it to the purposes of a particular party . . . or rather the leaders of a party". After the death of Lenin, he further wrote that "even with the best intentions he was a tyrant who strangled the Russian revolution — and we who could not admire him while alive, cannot mourn him now he is dead. Lenin is dead. Long live Liberty . . ."'

Diary of Christina Donato:

'I roam in search of Carlo. All the radicals in New York City are hiding or have been arrested; meeting halls are being raided, literature and records confiscated. My ageing uncle has been deported. He is man in his seventies and of ill-health, treated like a criminal. Several people have seen Carlo, but none know his whereabouts. It is reported that he has been arrested, but this is false. I call upon an old-timer who refuses to speak to me until he learns I am the mother of Carlo's child and divulges that Carlo has left the city, but that is all he can say. I stay with my cousin but it is not safe and I cannot place her family in a compromising position. She avoids politics altogether. There is another raid while I am in the city; several dozen immigrants, mostly Russians and Italians, are arrested. There's nothing left for us to do but flee to Italy. Best to go on our own volition than be arrested and deported. Emma is a citizen. I can leave her here or take her with me. My cousin has offered to take her if necessary but I cannot let her go. I borrow money from my cousin for my return to Boston. Once there I will go to Carlo's mother's. He will be there I am certain. Emma is stricken with a virus and is too sick to travel. I wait out her illness. My cousin and her husband are nervous and each time footsteps can be heard in the hall they wince, but they have not the heart to put me and the baby out. With the first sign of improvement in Emma, we depart. In the meantime, I make daily inquiries around the neighborhood. I return to the old man but he has been arrested.'

The Notebooks

'... What happened in Washington last night in the attempt upon the Attorney General's life is but a symptom of the terrible unrest that is stalking about the country ... As a Democrat I would be disappointed to see the Republican Party gain power. That is not what depresses one so much as to see growing steadily from day to day, under our very eyes, a movement that, if it is not checked, is bound to express itself in attack upon everything we hold dear. In this era of industrial and social unrest both parties are in disrepute with the average man ... The identity of the bomber is still unknown. The body was blown into so many pieces bits of flesh were found a block away, along with debris from the Attorney General's home. A federal official reported that identification from the remains might be impossible...'

The Notebooks

'... Pains were taken to give spectacular publicity to the raid, and to make it appear that there was great and public imminent danger ... The arrested aliens, in most instances perfectly quiet and harmless working people ... were handcuffed in pairs, and then, for the purposes of transfer on trains and through the streets of Boston, chained together ... We had words, we had music, we had poetry. *L'estetica*, Galleani told us, is always part of *la politica*. We were so happy, and young. Tina, Fillipo, Irma and Rizieri. Ella – they called her the dynamite girl when they caught her in Chicago with dynamite under her skirts. And then there was Carlo. He could do everything. Handsome, a poet, an editor. But he felt too deep. He felt the hypocrisy of the world too strong. Attorney General Palmer – he claimed to be a Quaker; but he declared war against radical America. He broke up so many families and ruined so many lives. Too much hypocrisy. What we needed was plain words. Plain words was what Carlo wanted to say when he brought the package and tripped going up the stairs ...'

Diary of Christina Donato:

'It is dark. They wake us and we gather up our things. Emma is at my breast in the middle of feeding but I must pry her away as there is no time. We are rushed out of our holding cells and marched outside into a yard. A rain blows hard and we stand single file shivering with federal agents on each side who march us to the water past rows of armed soldiers lining the road. The soldiers curse and threaten us as we pass carrying our meager bundles. Some of the women are sobbing. Emma is crying for milk and I hold her tight against me with one arm and clutch my heavy bag in the other. We reach the water's edge and I see the dark shape of a barge against the blacker water. The agents order us across the plank, and one by one we step up and cross it. Soldiers with fixed bayonets line the deck and herd the women into a large cabin where there are not enough benches for us all to sit; the oldest women take the benches but I am offered a seat so that I may finish feeding Emma. The men remain out in the rain on the open deck, many of them without clothing fit for such conditions. Suddenly the barge lurches forward and we slip away from the mooring. Somewhere out on the open water is a bigger ship where they will take us. There is a fire in a large stove burning in the middle of the cabin but it is too hot, the room feels suffocating and the air is foul. Women stare straight ahead with blank watery eyes. Others bury their faces in their hands. Emma finishes her feeding and I offer my seat to a woman who is sick on her feet. I look out the porthole above the heads of the men and soldiers. The New York skyline slides by in a rainy glass blur. We chug out past the Statue of Liberty. Everything is dark except for the light of her torch.

■■■

When the stewardess came around and handed me a copy of *The New York Times*, the first article I noticed on the front page regarded someone called the Unabomber, as of yet unidentified, suspected of being responsible for several mail-bombs over the years. As I read the article and learned more of the Unabomber, my first thought was it's Vin. I don't know why; as far as I knew, Vin had no knowledge of explosives. I had never seen him with anything that might resemble literature on explosives in his apartment. But where did he go all of those long days? What about all of the phone calls from his 'contacts' around the world? His trips to Mexico? Vin wasn't capable of such an act.

I slept through most of the flight, and when the pilot announced that we would be landing at Logan International Airport within several minutes, I looked out the window to see the Mystic River Bridge and Boston alight. I thought it might feel good to see home but I felt nothing. No loved one would greet me as I walked off of the plane, and I still wasn't sure where I would go. The only person I felt any connection with was Vin, and I left the country without saying good-bye to him. I followed the crowd to the baggage-claim area, walked out through the electric swinging doors and hailed a taxi. The driver asked where to, and I gave him Vin's address.

It was after midnight when the taxi pulled up in front of Vin's. The rooms were dark but Vin's car was in the driveway. I paid the driver, grabbed my bag out of the trunk and climbed the stairs. I gave the door a hard knock. There was no answer so I knocked again, then rang the bell. Several more knocks and bell-rings went unanswered so I picked up my bag and started down the stairs and just then I noticed movement at the front window.

The front door opened and a woman's voice called out my name. Veronica. She ran down the stairs in a night shirt and underpants and threw her arms around me.

'Greg. Greg,' tears rolling down her face. 'Where have you been?'

'What do you mean where have I been? I've been in Italy. Where's Vin?'

'Oh Christ.'

She took me by the arm and led me up the stairs into the apartment. In the kitchen she put on a pot of espresso, holding back sobs. I looked around the apartment. It was a mess. Books, records, papers were strewn haphazardly over the floor.

'Do you want a drink?'

'Yeah, but where the fuck is Vin?'

'He's dead. Vin's dead.'

I tried to speak but couldn't. I swallowed. 'Dead?'

She placed the pot of espresso and two cups on to the dining-room table, walked over to me and we embraced. Her tears began again.

'I loved him, you know. I really loved him. Everything happened so fast. Didn't you hear about the computer ring?'

'I don't know what you're talking about.'

Veronica sat down at the table and wiped her tears on her shirtsleeve. Then she began to speak. Shortly after I left for Italy, Vin began to suffer from various physical symptoms which, in his usual fashion, he ignored. He lost weight and his appetite and his extraordinary energy level diminished. His skin color got real bad and he was suffering from assorted pains. Veronica urged him to see a doctor but he refused, claiming that he was the victim of a bug and it would pass. As usual, he indulged in the medicine that he used whenever he suffered a common cold or major flu – grappa. One morning he collapsed on the living-room floor. Veronica phoned for an ambulance and they rushed Vin to the hospital. Against Vin's wishes they held him there for tests; within a few days he was diagnosed with liver cancer. They gave him six months, give or take. Vin took it well, a lot better than Veronica. During that time she did everything she could to make him comfortable, though he insisted on working when he felt up to it.

Suddenly one morning federal agents appeared at the door and arrested Vin in connection with a ring which was distributing illegal computer programs. The programs were used to sabotage computer systems. At one point a virus made its way into the Pentagon's main computer system and only a turn of fate and some quick action on the part of the Pentagon's computer aces destroyed it. The virus was said to work by stealing information while it simultaneously deleted it from the target system. The story was in the national headlines for several days. The ring originated somewhere overseas, possibly Pakistan, and the central connection on the American continent was in Mexico. Veronica said that she had no idea what Vin was involved in, but when she visited him in jail he didn't deny it.

Vin was quite knowledgeable about computers, but he was no hacker. At the same time I didn't doubt for an instant he might somehow be connected to such an operation. It all made sense. Vin's bail was set too high for Veronica to raise the money. She was in the process of securing the official medical records to prove Vin's illness which might allow him to be released until trial when she got a call from someone who told her Vin died in his sleep. She went to the morgue with Vin's brother. Vin had left wishes to have his body cremated. There was no money so his brother provided the fee. She pointed to the liquor cabinet and said he's in that blue jar.

In the meantime agents visited Vin's apartment several times and turned it inside out. They took every computer disc, all of the micro-film archive and projector, all of Vin's files, papers and notebooks regardless of whether they reflected on the case. They pulled down all books from the shelves, opened each one to inspect them for secret compartments, emptied record covers of their contents on the floor, and left everything where it fell. On two occasions Veronica was brought in for questioning. My name came up in each interrogation, and the feds flashed a driver's license photo of me wanting to know my whereabouts. If I wasn't connected with the ring Veronica said, it would be best I contact the agents and clear myself now that I was back in the country. If I was involved, then I should get myself a good lawyer.

She said in the months Vin was ill, he spoke of me often and desperately hoped that I would return before he died. He was sorry things turned out the way they did. Knowing I would eventually return, Vin left his archive and library to me. He told Veronica that I would know what to do with everything. But except for the trashed books, albums and tapes – all the archival work was confiscated. Every last bit of film, all of the files and discs, a lifetime of Vin's work, gone.